"I don't intend to be cheated," he told her

Mal's gaze was fixed upon her face as he spoke. "I want the d'Arth name carried on now that the foundry and château are at last mine."

He extended a hand to her and drew her to her feet. Glenda felt the hard encirclement of his arms as he pressed her body to his, and she shuddered.

His fingers gripped her chin and forced her face up. "I'm damned if I'll have you afraid of me," he said. "I want no coward for a wife or son."

"I'm not afraid of you," she denied. "I wouldn't give you that satisfaction."

"No, there are other kinds of satisfaction I'd prefer from you." Abruptly he lowered his head and his lips fastened on hers in a devastating kiss.

D0181053

VIOLET WINSPEAR
is also the author of these

Harlequin Presents

and these

Harlequin Romances

Many of these books are available at your local bookseller.

For a free catalog listing all titles currently available,
send your name and address to:

HARLEQUIN READER SERVICE
1440 South Priest Drive, Tempe, AZ 85281
Canadian address: Stratford, Ontario N5A 6W2

CS

VIOLET
WINSPEAR

the man she married

Harlequin Books

TORONTO • NEW YORK • LOS ANGELES • LONDON
AMSTERDAM • PARIS • SYDNEY • HAMBURG
STOCKHOLM • ATHENS • TOKYO • MILAN

Harlequin Presents first edition January 1983
ISBN 0-373-10566-5

Original hardcover edition published in 1982
by Mills & Boon Limited

Copyright © 1982 by Violet Winspear. All rights reserved.
Philippine copyright 1982. Australian copyright 1982.
Except for use in any review, the reproduction or utilization
of this work in whole or in part in any form by any electronic,
mechanical or other means, now known or hereafter invented,
including xerography, photocopying and recording, or in any
information storage or retrieval system, is forbidden without
the permission of the publisher, Harlequin Enterprises Limited,
225 Duncan Mill Road, Don Mills, Ontario, Canada M3B 3K9.

All the characters in this book have no existence outside the
imagination of the author and have no relation whatsoever to
anyone bearing the same name or names. They are not even
distantly inspired by any individual known or unknown to the
author, and all the incidents are pure invention.

The Harlequin trademarks, consisting of the words
HARLEQUIN PRESENTS and the portrayal of a Harlequin,
are trademarks of Harlequin Enterprises Limited and are
registered in the Canada Trade Marks Office; the portrayal
of a Harlequin is registered in the United States Patent
and Trademark Office.

Printed in U.S.A.

'Twist ye, twine ye! even so
Mingle shades of joy and woe,
Hope and fear, and peace, and strife,
In the thread of human life.

Now they wax, and now they dwindle,
Whirling with the whirling spindle.
Twist ye, twine ye! even so
Mingle human bliss and woe.'

Sir Walter Scott, *Guy Mannering*

CHAPTER ONE

PHOTOGRAPHERS were there, and the people of Barton-le-Cross hadn't seen a wedding like it for years.

Of course, they murmured, it was a pity the bride's mother hadn't lived long enough to see Glenda married. Edith Hartwell would have felt so proud of her daughter in the white slipper satin dress, with a lovely lace veil covering her face.

As the bride entered the church the photographers pleaded with her to throw back her veil so they could take pictures of her face, but she resisted their pleas and proceeded along the aisle on the arm of Sir Arthur Brake, who had been a close friend of her mother's, and when they reached the altar Glenda still left the veil in place.

The ceremony had an unreal quality for her, and being here in the fine old Norman church was a sad reminder of a service quite different from this one.

It had rained that day, the miserable drops of rain mingling with the tears on her face as Edith's coffin was lowered into the deep, shadowy soil. Since she was a child of ten Glenda had lived with Edith, and everyone believed them to have been mother and daughter.

Everybody in church today believed they were seeing the marriage of Edith Hartwell's daughter to Malraux d'Ath. Only Glenda and Sir Arthur knew the real truth . . . that Edith's real daughter had died nine years ago and was buried on the island of Malta.

'How do I go through with it?' Glenda had pleaded of Sir Arthur.

'You go through with it, m'dear, because you loved that woman, and because you promised her you would. Edie had her faults, but she was good to you, and if you refuse to marry d'Ath you'll be breaking your word to her. Don't ever forget that she took you out of that children's home up there in Llandudno and gave you advantages you would never have had otherwise.'

In a kind of dream that bordered on a nightmare Glenda made her responses at the tall, dark side of Malraux d'Ath. When he slid the gold ring on to her finger she felt his eyes probing the veil which she felt compelled to hide behind.

He believed he was marrying the girl chosen for him a decade ago by the dying old patriarch Duval Malraux who had joined a schoolgirl's hand to his grandson's and demanded of them a promise so similar to the one Edith had asked of Glenda.

'I've deceived the old man's family all these years.' Edith's pain that day had been worse than Glenda had ever seen it, but she had refused her medication until she extracted from Glenda the promise which today was being fulfilled in front of a congregation and a man in holy vestments. Because Glenda had loved Edith like a mother she took as her husband a man she didn't love . . . a man she barely knew.

'I never told Malraux's family that my real girl died while we were on a cruise and that her burial took place in Malta.' The words had scraped painfully out of Edith's wasted throat. 'They'd have cut off my allowance, you see. How was I to live? I'd never worked, and that old reprobate paid the allowance because he had it all planned that my daughter should marry his grandson.'

The organ music pealed and on the arm of Malraux

d'Ath a pale and trembling Glenda went with him to sign the marriage register. Although Mal had a French mother he had been born in England and, in a few moments when they signed their names they would be man and wife, for better, for worse.

And Glenda knew today why Edith had taken the trouble soon after she had taken her from that orphanage in Llandudno to have her name legally changed to Hartwell and with that beguiling smile of hers had asked the thin-faced, shy and gawky child if she would object to having as her first name the pretty name of Glenda.

How could any child have resisted such a woman, clad in furs to her huge green eyes and smelling so deliciously of a Lakeland bouquet perfume she had always worn, from the first day she took Glenda home with her in a big black Rolls-Royce until the day she died in a lamplit hospital room.

The pen almost slid from Glenda's uncertain hand as she wrote her name beneath the slashing dark signature of the tall and powerful man in his superb grey suit. Malraux Armand d'Ath—a name as forceful and distinguished as the man himself. The man who was unaware that he had married an impostor.

'Put back your veil,' he ordered suddenly. 'The people out there will want to see your face.'

It was then that Glenda slid to the floor in a dead faint, unaware until later that it was Sir Arthur who came to her rescue with all the diplomacy at his command. 'Don't forget,' he said to the groom,' that the poor girl only recently suffered the sad loss of her mother. They were constantly together, and Edith was a loving woman towards the child. I know just how brave Glenda has been today—she has braved the fact that

Edith couldn't be here to see her married.'

By the time Glenda and her husband arrived at the airport she was feeling physically better because the champagne had buoyed her up; but when Mal touched a hand to her waist as they boarded the jet plane, she felt her nerves tighten up. They were bound for Angervilliers and his château on the Loire.

Soon after the plane took off Glenda went to the ladies' room in order to remove some grains of rice which had slipped down the neck of her silky georgette blouse. She stared at her face in a mirror and wondered if Mal had noticed that her pallor intensified the amber flecks in her eyes, making them seem like flashes of wild fire.

A cold shiver ran up and down her spine despite the warmth of the powder-room, the luxury of it here on the streamlined deck of the great airliner.

An hour ago her body had been clad in elegant silk and a certain courage had been hers. When the Rector had pronounced those words, 'I require and charge you both, as ye will answer at the dreadful day of judgment, when the secrets of all hearts shall be disclosed, that if either of you know any impediment, why ye may not be lawfully joined together in Matrimony, ye do now confess it,' her heart's blood had run cold, and it had only been courage which had upheld her until she reached the vestry where they had signed the register.

Glenda knew she had fainted from fear and guilt, for there was something about Malraux d'Ath which warned her he could be cruel if his trust in anyone was betrayed. In marrying him that was exactly what she had done—betrayed him. In repaying her debt of gratitude to Edith Hartwell she had led him up the aisle, and she didn't want to imagine what he'd do to her if he found out.

She glanced at the ring on her left hand and recalled that petrifying moment at the altar when the best man had laid the ring of gold upon the prayer book and Mal had gazed right through her veil before slipping the ring on to her bridal finger. What had been his thoughts at that moment? Did he resent a bride who had been chosen for him? There was an English side to him that might find the Latin arrangement hard to take.

Glenda clenched her hand until her fingernails dug into her flesh. How much harder he would take it if he ever found out that she wasn't the girl whose hand had been placed in his across the bed of his dying grandfather.

Instead she was a foundling whom Edith Hartwell had adopted, choosing her from dozens of other ten-year-olds because she had the white Welsh skin that her daughter had, and the dark red hair that was such a contrast to such skin.

The only noticeable difference lay in the eyes. The dead girl's eyes had been a deep green like her mother's.

Glenda held her own amber gaze in the powder-room mirror and felt the frightened beat of her heart. She would really be in trouble if Malraux d'Ath had a good memory for such details. It had been ten years since the marriage had been arranged, so she must hope that he wouldn't remember that the girl chosen for him had green eyes without a fragment of amber in them.

Strange, she told herself, that he had kept away from Barton-le-Cross all that time; from the white house on the hill which had been Glenda's home since her adoption. Edith had moved right away from Chelsea and all her old haunts and the people they became friendly with at Barton-le-Cross were never aware that they weren't tied by blood to each other. The only person Edith had confided in had been Sir Arthur Brake, whom as Glenda grew up she renamed Rake.

A good-humoured old rake who had probably encouraged Edith in her deception. He would have known the size of the allowance given to Edith by the d'Ath family, to whom her husband had been related. Kind, affectionate, extravagant Edith, ensuring that Glenda had all the advantages of a good upbringing and education; taking her with her on her travels as she grew up and her Celtic colouring intensified. Girls changed as they grew older, Edith reasoned, so if they ran into any of her old friends they would only notice the skin and the hair and the obvious affection that Glenda and Edith had for each other.

It had not been possible for Glenda to refuse to go through with the marriage which had taken place today. Edith had clung to her hand and begged it of her.

'Don't let me die a thief in their eyes,' she had pleaded. 'The d'Aths are rich, but they're proud, and not a soul but Arthur knows that my other Glenda is buried on that island. Do it for me, darling. It will only be a white lie.'

But the lie wasn't a white one . . . it was as dark and unpredictable as the man with whom she was now involved. A man who would be well within his rights to put his hands around her neck and choke her if he found out that she wasn't the girl he believed her to be. Instead her real identity was unknown; she was someone who had been abandoned as a baby by her real mother.

Gathering together the shreds of her courage, Glenda made her way along the aisle of the plane, clad in an ivory-coloured suit and wearing a hat with the brim pulled down at a rakish angle, shading her eyes. All day long she had felt an inclination to hide her face, and she could hardly bring herself to sit down at the side of the man she had married in the guise of a girl who had died a year after his engagement to her.

That untimely death should have released him from the marriage his grandfather had wanted, but because Edith Hartwell had wanted to go on living well at the expense of Duval Malraux, his grandson was now the husband of a shameful liar.

There was no other way to think of it, no escape for Glenda from her guilt feeling. She had known of the arrangement. Edith had spoken of it, but in a light, dismissive way which had made Glenda believe that Mal would be told the truth about her adoption before any plans for a marriage were solidified.

Then Edith had started to get ill; she had undergone an operation which had eased her for a while. The latter stages of her illness had taken a rapid course and before Glenda could protest she had found herself conspiring with a dying woman to conceal the way in which Edith had defrauded Mal and his family.

'He won't be any the wiser,' Edith had said in that heartrending voice that barely scraped its way out of her throat. 'French people think nothing of the arranged marriage, and Mal is French on his mother's side. And you, dearest Glen, you've been like a real daughter to me. You and I have been happy together, haven't we?'

It was true, those years with Edith had been happy

ones, but as Glenda accepted a glass of wine from Mal and felt his steely eyes probing her face, it seemed as if happiness was something she would never know again. She felt like a scarlet sinner but looked pale as the white flowers she had carried to the altar and which in the vestry she had crushed when she had fallen upon them.

Her faintness had been put down to nerves and the strain of Edith's illness, but Glenda knew the real truth. She had married a dark foreign stranger, and it terrified her to have to think of him as her husband.

'Drink up,' he urged. 'You're still looking rather pale—brides don't usually pass out at a man's feet. Was it caused by an excess of emotion, do you think?'

She managed a brief smile as she tilted her glass and took a deep swallow of the wine.

'We have to get to know each other, don't we?' Mal added. 'It couldn't have been easy for you, marrying a stranger. Well, almost a stranger—we did meet when you were a starry-eyed youngster, didn't we?'

She drank some more of her wine and didn't dare to look at him. Then, before she could stop him, he removed her hat and tossed it to one side.

'That's better, now I can see your face. Glenda, you've grown up to be rather shy, haven't you? I remember you as a pert young miss who made eyes at me.'

As Mal spoke his eyes raked over her silky red hair. His gaze settled on her mouth, softly scarlet against her white skin. There was a winged look to her brows, and the sunlight through the windows had filtered into her eyes and lit those fragments of amber.

'I seem also to remember the long eyelashes,' he murmured.

Glenda returned his look with a rather distracted one. She watched the play of his fingers upon the bowl and stem of his wine glass . . . fingers lean yet strong, that might just as easily snap a woman's neck as caress it.

'It is difficult, isn't it, for a pair of strangers to feel married,' he said, quirking a black eyebrow. 'I don't wonder that all the vow making made you feel faint— you feel a little stronger now?'

'I'm trying to,' she rejoined. 'It—it might have made things easier, *monsieur*, had you ever visited us before Edith—before my mother died. Why didn't you?'

'Because of this.' He touched a hand to the left side of his face. 'I looked different when we met ten years ago. This happened two years ago in a fire at one of our factories, so I thought it best to let *une petite fille* remember me when I was better looking.'

Glenda gazed at the hard, half-savage bones under the brazen tan of his skin where the fire scars bit deep into his left profile. Yes, at one time he would have been more good-looking, but where the scars twisted his lip and pulled at his eye there was a distortion that was more sinister than ugly.

'Did it hurt?' The rather childlike question left her lips before she could stop it. She flushed and lowered her gaze. 'What a silly thing to say! It must have hurt like hell!'

'So it did.' Cigar smoke drifted from his lips and the aroma teased her nostrils. 'Was it my scars that gave you a shock when we faced each other as man and wife? Did you realise then that you are going to have to live with them?'

'I—I'm not a child,' she blurted. 'Not any more.'

'No, perhaps not.' His gaze raked over her. 'If you

are wondering why I haven't resorted to cosmetic surgery, *ma chérie*, it's because very little can be done to
eradicate the damage in my case, even apart from the fact
that I'm not prepared to undergo spells on my back
while a surgeon hacks away at me. I always had less
flesh than bone in my face and was never a matinée
idol——'

'Please,' Glenda broke in, 'it isn't your scars that
worry me——'

'You feel a lack of romance, eh, in having married a
veritable stranger?'

'Yes.' She inclined her head, her hair shimmering in
the sunlight.

'Never mind!' He gave a slightly mocking laugh. 'All
that will change when I get you to the Château Noir.'

'I beg of you——' Her words were barely audible
above the pounding of her heart. She felt sick with
shame for having deceived him and taken him in by
her deception. Could marriage vows be regarded as
sacred if a bride stood at the altar in a dead girl's shoes?
How on earth did she ever begin to feel like his wife?
When would she ever stop feeling like a fraud who
expected at any moment to be exposed and punished?

Glenda had no idea how stricken was the look in her
eyes as she faced Mal d'Ath and saw in him a kind of
ruthlessness that would make it impossible for him not
to go through with whatever he started. He wouldn't
withdraw a kind word or a cruel one. If he broke a
woman's heart he would do it completely.

'You are asking me to give you time, eh?' Cigar
smoke eddied from his lips. 'Time to get to know me
as a husband?'

'I need——' Her right hand clenched over her left
one; she had put down her wine glass on the table,

afraid of dropping it from nerveless fingers.

'But we always knew, you and I, that we would have to face this day together.' His eyes had the glint of steel from beneath narrowed eyelids. 'At no time did your mother ever contact me to say that you felt—reluctant, shall I say? This was always possible, but the years went by and I had no indication from either of you that the marriage wouldn't take place as planned, when you became twenty. The time for pleading, my dear, was before you stood at that altar beside me and gave yourself into my hands.'

Abruptly he set aside his own wine glass and as she watched in tongue-tied silence he reached into a pocket of his grey suit and withdrew a small square box. He flicked it open and instantly the sunlight was trapped in the heart-shaped diamond set in a circle of gold.

'This ring belonged to my grandmother,' he said. 'It must now join your wedding ring.'

'No——'

'Yes, Glenda.' He caught hold of her hand and she felt the power in his grip. She wanted to resist him, but instinct warned her that it was wiser to submit as he slid the diamond ring on to her finger, where it glittered and gleamed with the lustre of a genuine and very fine stone, most beautifully cut and shaped.

Watching her, Mal slowly raised her ringed hand to his lips and kissed the palm of it. 'In France that is where a man kisses intimately,' he murmured. 'The back of the hand is reserved for female relatives and friends. One's wife is a separate matter, and you are my wife, Glenda. We are joined together, for better, for worse, and thereto I gave thee my troth, as you gave me yours.'

The trembling she had felt at the altar was back, but

it was too late now to turn and run out of the church. She had almost done it. The courage had almost been hers when the Rector had asked if they should not be lawfully joined together.

'Don't you like your ring, *ma chérie?*' His fingers tightened on hers. 'After I went to the trouble to have the setting changed to suit you?'

'How could you know it would suit me?' Her voice was low and tense. 'You never came to Barton-le-Cross, and I could have grown up to be—different from what you remembered. Girls change.'

'The colour of your hair couldn't change.' He lounged back in his seat and his smile twisted oddly on his lips. 'It was braided down over your shoulder that day my grandfather took our hands and joined them together across his sickbed. Stabs of sunlight came through the stained glass windows of his room and your braided hair was alive, like a flame against your white skin. Those attributes haven't changed, *ma chérie*, but you have grown less exuberant at the idea of being the mistress of the Château Noir. Perhaps when you see the Château again you will regain some of your former delight in the idea of living there.'

'I—it will seem strange to me after so long a time,' she managed to say.

'I expect so,' he agreed. 'So the braid is gone and the red hair is modishly cut and styled. You have grown most attractive, Glenda, and yet you are somehow different from what I imagined. Have I lived too long with the image of "a wicked white Magdalen"?'

Her heart tripped at what he said. 'You sound—disappointed in me,' she murmured, not meaning to sound provoking, but her voice had a natural faint huskiness, an alluring quality which echoed the Welsh blood in her veins.

He leaned towards her and his eyes in his scarred face were like shaded silver. 'I don't quite know what my feelings are with regard to you, Glenda. I certainly never expected you to faint at my feet—that was the very last thing I expected of the composed child who came to Angervilliers all those years ago and wasn't in the least disturbed by the idea of being engaged to a young man already at college. When my grandfather told you to kiss me, you made play with those absurdly long lashes and quite eagerly kissed my cheek, but as I wasn't scarred in those days, there was nothing for you to be scared of.'

'It isn't your scars.' She lowered her lashes, shielding her eyes that would never remember him as a good-looking youth of nineteen. 'Uncle Arthur explained to you that I—I'm still not over the death of my mother. I loved her very much.'

'Of course,' he said, and she tried not to shrink away as he touched a finger to her cheek and drew his fingertip down the slope of her cheekbone to the corner of her mouth. 'I know how I felt when I lost Grandpère; he raised me after my parents were killed on their farm in Algiers—a petrol bomb was flung into their sitting-room and they were unable to escape the blaze. I was more fortunate when my factory was burned. I emerged alive, but the scars aren't pretty, I realise that, even though you protest that they don't repel you.'

'They don't,' she repeated. And yet she wasn't sure, for they gave him a sinister look abetted by hair and brows as black as sin.

'Ah well,' he shrugged, 'there are always things that

we mortally fear, like pain and death . . . and love's retribution.'

'Retribution?' She echoed the word painfully.

'We have married, have we not, to appease love of a kind—the selfish love of the ones who cared for us when we were young. Neither of us fought their dictate, did we? We are married, you and I, and now we have to make the best of it.'

Glenda sat there silently, permitting him to refill her wine glass but shaking her head at the smoked salmon. She couldn't bring herself to eat anything, though she agreed silently with his warning that the wine would go to her head if she didn't eat. Let the wine muzz her thoughts and numb her sensations of guilt. Perhaps it would also help her to feel brave when the time came for her to enter the Château Noir as its mistress.

She hoped it wasn't a large and awesome place, with a retinue of domestics and a routine which she would have to deal with. She and Edith had lived comfortably at Barton-le-Cross, but Glenda wasn't used to running a large establishment and giving orders to a butler and various maids.

With a desperate need to bolster her courage she drank her wine, and was aware of her husband watching her intently through the smoke of his cigar.

How was she going to live with a stranger who had every right to be more intimate with her than anyone she had ever known before? Edith had kept a vigilant eye upon her, but by her own choice she had not been a girl to experiment with love. She had been more interested in the places they had visited than in the men who felt an inclination to approach her. She had given them only a cool response which had quickly cooled their ardour.

She had gained a reputation among Edith's friends for being a devoted daughter. But being a devoted daughter was different from being a wife who felt afraid of the man she had married.

CHAPTER TWO

AWAITING them at the airport was a sleek brown car with cognac upholstery, white-rimmed wheels and a powerful engine under the hood, which Mal drove with controlled speed along the highway that gradually elevated until the Loire had become a satin ribbon far beneath them.

Glenda was glad of the car ride; it gave her a margin of time in which to gather herself together in order to face her first meeting with those members of the Malraux family residing at the Château.

The sky was filling with the sun's last blaze as they came in sight of Mal's birthplace and Glenda saw the Château Noir silhouetted against the burning sky, its dark-silver walls overlaid by a sheen of flaming gold as the sun died away.

There it stood, perched upon its own summit above the fascinating Loire valley, a sprawl of pepperpot roofs, cobbled walls and courtyards concealed behind shawls of ivy. Oval-shaped windows were set deeply in the curve of the twin towers with their witch-like black peaks and each tower had its own battlement. Centred between the towers was the main bulk of the Château, graciously weathered and four storeys high, lights to be seen here and there against the silvery stonework, evidence of people preparing for dinner behind the long windows with their narrow balconies of wrought-iron.

It was upon iron that the fortunes of this family had been founded long ago. This was one of the great iron-foundry families of France and responsible for some of the finest wrought-iron to be seen in Paris and London and other great cities. In wartime London there had been destruction of much of the original ironwork designed by the Malraux Foundry, and it was Mal's grandfather who had set to work to replace it. Mal carried on the family tradition in partnership with one of his cousins, overseeing the factories in England while his cousin Matthieu took care of the French side of the business.

'Impressed?' Mal turned to face Glenda as the car's engine stilled and they were for a few moments more alone together.

'It takes my breath away,' she replied.

'I heard you catch your breath, so I take it you had forgotten how it looked.'

'Yes.' She bit her lip. 'Ten years is a long time.'

'And you return a veritable stranger to the place that will now be your home.'

Home . . . it was a word with warmth and welcome in it, but for Glenda it was haunted by the terrors that chilled her heart.

'Be tranquil,' Mal murmured. 'I shan't put you through the ordeal of a family dinner tonight. You no doubt crave a bath, and then we shall have *diner* alone together and share a bottle of Puligny-Montrachet from the cache that was put down for me by my grandfather. He was not a champagne man and he taught me to appreciate the wine he most liked. The wine and the woman, it would seem.'

Glenda pressed her hands together and felt the pressure of the rings that were golden bands of bondage so far as she was concerned. 'I am his choice, not yours, so do you feel—resentful?' she asked nervously.

'At this moment in time, *chérie*, we don't explore our feelings, we just let life happen to us. Come, let us go indoors.'

He slid from his own side of the car and came round to open the door beside Glenda. Her legs were trembling as she emerged and stood there beneath the double flight of steps that led up to the entrance.

'*L'oiseau crie trop tard quand il est pris.*' Mal gazed down at her, her ringed hand lost in his.

So he knew exactly how she felt; she was like a bird crying out too late in the trap.

He smiled briefly, his scarred lip twisting. '*Qui ne dit mot consent, chérie.*'

Yes, her silence had answered him. She wasn't going to deny it.

'All the same,' he resumed in English, 'a pleasant trap. The Château Noir is considered quite a feast for the eyes, despite being called a black castle.'

'The stonework has a silvery sheen.' She gazed up the side of one of the towers to the battlement; from up there one would see over half the countryside.

'The name of the Château refers to some of its original history,' Mal informed her. 'As you are aware, the Malraux family came by it through industry and not nobility, and legend has it that a sinister lord lived here with his favoured mistress, reputed to be a young witch. When she fell out of favour with him, he had her burned.'

'How awful!' Glenda exclaimed. 'Is it true?'

'It's recorded in an old volume which came with the Château when it became Malraux property. Superstition was rife in those days—there's even a small portrait which depicts the girl. Have you forgotten?'

'Forgotten?' Glenda gazed up into Mal's eyes and saw the look they held in the light that came from a scrolled lantern attached to a nearby wall. That look was curious—speculative.

'You seem,' he said, 'to have wiped from your mind quite a few of the things you found so intriguing the last time you were here. Grandpère had that portrait hanging on the wall of his room, and he remarked that the girl reminded him of you.'

'Me!'

'She, too, had hair like dark fire and slant eyes against white skin.'

Glenda felt her throat go dry and was near petrified when Mal suddenly gripped her by the chin and searched her eyes. 'I've been wondering all day—ah well, as you said, *ma chérie*, ten years is a long time and time not only changes us, it changes our perspective. Then you were a schoolgirl with a head filled with romantic nonsense, but now you are a woman and nervous of me, eh?'

She didn't deny it; he was standing close enough to feel her trembling with nerves.

'Have you married me against your will?' he demanded. 'Has this day been such an ordeal for you?'

'It can't have been easy for you,' she rejoined, 'marrying a woman you aren't in love with.'

'Love?' He spoke the word mockingly. 'All I know is how to take hold of hot iron and shape it to my demands, and I shall do the same with you. *Bon gré, mal gré!*'

'Whether I like it or not?' she echoed. 'God, is that the kind of man you are?'

'All men are that kind.'

Glenda stared up at him and his darkness and his scars cloaked him in a sinister aura. Oh God, now she saw that she *had* married a man who resented her even as they stood on the threshold of the home they must share. The strength and texture of iron had ruled his life, and that promise made to his grandfather had been too iron-bound for him to break.

She was a different matter; she was made of flesh and bone and easier to break . . . a cry escaped her as Mal swept her up in his arms and carried her into the Château, past the manservant who stood holding open the door.

'Here we are, André. I bring home my wife.'

'Welcome home, *monsieur et madame.*'

'We shall have dinner in my apartment, André. Inform my Aunt Héloise of this; she has been well in my absence?'

'Quite as usual, *monsieur*. Her hip troubles her, but she doesn't complain too much, except to the gardeners.'

'Ah yes.' Mal smiled in his sardonic way. 'She would much prefer to dig in the flowerbeds herself. I trust that something rather special is being prepared for dinner? Also I should like a bottle of Puligny-Montrachet brought to us.'

'I shall see to it, *monsieur.*'

'And send one of the girls to assist Madame with her *toilette*.'

Glenda tensed in his arms and wanted to protest that she could very well manage her own *toilette*. He quickly sensed this, and as he strode with her across the wide hall to an arched doorway and a stairway beyond, he said in curt tones:

'It may seem to your British mind an extravagance to have a maid to wait upon you, but it's part of our way of life here at the Château Noir and my aunt would be scandalized if you flouted her expectations. She would have been at our wedding, but travel has become difficult for her since she broke her hip last year. You won't recall her. She wasn't resident here at the Château in Grandpère's time; they didn't get on and apart from that she was managing her own fashion salon in Paris. She's the mother of my partner Matt.'

'I see.' Glenda felt the supple movement of his body as he mounted the twisting flight of stairs, carrying her as easily as if she were the weight of the schoolgirl who would have explored this house with the eager expectations of one day living here.

'My apartment is situated in the Tour Etoile where we shall live in *solitude à deux*; the expected preference of a newlywed couple, would you not say?'

Glenda was speechless, while he seemed barely out of breath as he carried her over the threshold of his *pied-à-terre*. He set her upon her feet but continued to keep his arms around her. She was very aware of the sinewy dark look of him, and it seemed to her that the iron in which he dealt had become part of him so that he wouldn't unbend to her fears and give her time to adjust to him as a husband.

'I think it time we kissed,' he said, in the deep half-Gallic tones that were as disturbing as everything else about him. 'That cool brush of the lips at the altar couldn't be called a kiss.'

Glenda met his eyes, and then she had to be cruel in order to protect herself. Deliberately she let her gaze rest upon his scars, then she shuddered in a most convincing manner and offered her mouth with a look of martyrdom on her face.

His arms hardened around her until they felt like bars of iron, rigid and bruising. He was looking down at her, searching her face, and then with a French oath he thrust her away from him.

'I knew you were lily-livered! I saw what you had changed into, but you'll change back, *ma chère*, and if you can't look at me in the light, then you'll just have to endure me in the dark!'

'No, Mal——' She gave him an agonised look. 'You owe me time to get to know you.'

'I owe you nothing.' He raked a hand through his black hair. 'Any debts of mine are paid up in full, and now I'm going to collect some interest—even if I have to force the lock in order to enjoy myself.'

'If I'm lily-livered,' she flung back at him, 'then you're as hard as iron!'

'Possibly so.' He shrugged his shoulders. 'I was led into the foundry at an early age and I could shape metal in the crucible by the time I was fourteen. It's my opinion that women, too, need to be melted and shaped to a man's demands. Especially you, my dear. You married the man that I am; you promised to cherish and honour me, didn't you?'

'You made the same promises, Mal.' Her voice shook, though she made an effort to control it. She didn't like feeling afraid of him, for Edith had done her best to instil self-confidence in her and to restore some of the ego which those early years in the orphanage had undermined. Few people realised what it meant to be a child who belonged to no one; whose home in the formative years was a grim old building still redolent of Victorian attitudes. Children had to obey rules, be grateful for the charity bestowed upon them, and never answer back to their betters.

Still the rules and regulations lingered in Glenda's mind, and even as she offered defiance to the man she had married, she realised that he had the right to her compliance.

'You won't see my face when the lights are out,' he said, and the scar beside his lips seemed to give the illusion of a snarl. 'The English have a saying, have they not . . . relax and think of your petit-point.'

'You're sarcastic, aren't you?' A flush ran over Glenda's skin. 'No one warned me of the man you— you had become.'

'At least I'm not telling you a pack of romantic lies,' he drawled. 'I'm not pretending that I adore you just to get you into a submissive attitude . . . or was it pretence that you hoped for?'

'As if I'd expect you to—to love a stranger?' She backed away from what his eyes were revealing now they were alone in his Tour Etoile, with no congregation to appease with an act of pretence; no airline hostess to notice the grains of rice that fell from his pocket when he showed their boarding card.

'Why did you come to Barton-le-Cross to marry me?' Glenda looked into eyes that were like smouldering steel. 'What was your real reason . . . there has to be one?'

'Why so, *ma chère*?'

'Because you aren't a sentimental man.'

'Can you bear to face the truth?' he mocked.

'I shall know where I stand, *monsieur*.'

'You stand upon ground sacred to me, *madame*. The Château Noir was to become mine if I kept my word to Duval Malraux, that old man of iron, otherwise it was to pass to my cousin Matt. Also a grandson, you realise, but the son of Héloise who disobeyed her father and ran off with a painter of dubious talent. Old Duval never forgave her; he was entrenched in the idea that the arranged marriage had more chance of survival than the so-called love match. Perhaps he was right. My aunt's marriage went on the rocks within three years, whereas my parents, whose union was arranged by Grandpère, were content together until terrorists killed them.'

He paused, his eyelids narrowing until his eyes seemed like slivers of steel.

'I admit to a lack of sentiment, *ma chère*, but all the same my grandfather gave me what affection he could spare, and he saw to it that I was steeped in his own lore of the iron foundry. He taught me all he had learned in his sixty-seven years. He trained me for the business and I had an aptitude for the foundry side of things, while Matt enjoyed the figure work. I felt that the Château was owed to me, and it didn't much concern me that in order to have it, I had to marry "the little white witch", as Grandpère called you.'

'I see.' Glenda spoke quietly, but she felt like screaming. She gazed with trapped eyes upon this man who didn't even pretend that she meant anything to him other than the means by which he secured this great pile of pinnacles and towers, with its history reaching back to the days when it was owned by a ruthless French lord who had burned his mistress for a witch when he lost interest in her as a woman.

'You asked for the truth,' said Mal, reading in her eyes her shocked reaction to his frankness. 'Come, *ma chère,* you must have suspected that I had more to gain from marrying you than the acquisition of a wife. You couldn't have supposed that I had my heart set on *you* all these years? I thought you a pretty enough child, and your unconcealed greed was amusing in those days. Do you still eat chocolates with such relish? Grandpère warned you that you'd get spots on your skin and I'd have to marry you with a veil over your face.'

His eyes scanned Glenda's face, with the flawless skin smooth and pale over the Celtic definition of her cheekbones. His eyes searched out the shadows under her cheekbones and there at her temples where her dark red hair was contoured.

'I don't see any spots, Glenda, so why did you keep your veil over your face?'

'So people wouldn't see me! Brides are supposed to look radiant, aren't they, Mal? I felt—tragic!'

'*Tragique* is a strong word to use, my dear, when you were being handed the keys of a castle. That's what you eagerly prattled on about as my grandfather enfolded our hands with his. You told him it had always been your dream to live in a castle on a hill and be like a princess in a tower.'

'Schoolgirls say such foolish things.' Suddenly Glenda felt such a sense of weakness that she had to sit down. It dawned on her that Edith's real daughter had been very unlike her beneath the skin. She sounded as if she had been precocious and far from shy, whereas Glenda had a lot of shyness in her, so that all the events of this wedding day had been an ordeal.

And the culmination was Mal's brazen admission that because he wanted the Château Noir he had married her to get it.

It had been at least bearable, believing that he went through with the marriage out of respect for a loved one's wishes. But he now assumed in her eyes the aspect of a mercenary, and when she looked at him, her aversion was in her gaze.

It was inevitable that he would misunderstand the reason for her look of aversion, and Glenda knew what he was thinking as he stood there tall and dark. He thought she shrank from his fire scars, obtained during an explosion at his London foundry. She knew he had been rushed to the burns unit at the East City hospital and though she felt sympathy for him in respect of the agony resulting from his burns, her sympathy did not include any basic understanding of him as a man.

He seemed to her as ruthless in his desires as the original master of the Château Noir . . . aptly named the black castle.

'I hope, *ma chérie*, that you haven't grown up to be one of those sickly, easily exhausted females who can be so depressing. As a schoolgirl you had plenty of zest, but today you have a fit of the vapours, and right now you look drained.'

Glenda sat there silently, recalling what Edith had imparted about her real daughter. It had not been outwardly evident that the girl had a heart condition, but suddenly on that Mediterranean cruise she had collapsed after playing a strenuous game of deck quoits followed by a lunch which had included a large helping of peaches and cream.

Mal had remarked on the girl's greed; her physical and emotional zest that would not have been good for someone with an underlying complaint of the heart.

Glenda thought to herself that if she was going to live a lie, then she might as well steep herself in it.

'Didn't you know?' she murmured. 'Did my mother conceal from your grandfather the fact that I have a rather weak heart?'

She heard him catch his breath and it was his turn to be silent while he absorbed her words. She had an idea what was passing through his mind as he towered darkly over her; the way she had trembled at the altar and then the way she had slid to the floor of the vestry in a dead faint. Aware of the natural whiteness of her skin, Glenda felt certain that she had looked ghostly when he had gathered her up in his arms. She knew he had done so, for when her eyes had fluttered open it was his face which she had seen above hers, and his arms had enclosed her as someone else held a glass of brandy and water to her lips. It would have been Sir Arthur who added the brandy from the flask he always carried, and brandy was recognised as a heart stimulant.

'*Dieu!*' Mal stared down at her, his brows drawn together in a frown. 'Your mother said not a word; no indication was given that you had any such thing wrong with you!'

'Well, does it really matter?' Glenda asked, and without conscious guile her fingers curled against her heart as she braved his steely look. 'The main thing is that you've got what you wanted, the Château.'

'*Madame,*' he sliced the air with the edge of his hand, 'don't pretend to be so innocent! I have a sound business which I want to pass on to a son, and I wanted the Château to be his when the time came, without any damned machinations! Do you understand me, or are you stupid as well as sickly?'

Glenda gazed appalled at him, for in his anger his scarred face had taken on a frightening look. His scars stood out lividly and fire seemed to burn in his eyes ... the way steel would glow in the furnace before being poured into the crucible.

'So we've both been cheated,' she said shakenly.

'You think so?' He spoke harshly. 'The getting of a son means a hell of a lot to me . . . you don't happen to mean half as much.'

His harsh statement sank into her mind like steel settling into the crucible where it was shaped so hard that only a return to the furnace would melt it down to be shaped anew.

'I—I never expected to mean anything to you,' she said huskily. 'I had only to look at you to see you for what you are.'

'And what am I, *madame*?'

'A man of iron, turned out in the same mould as Duval Malraux. He probably set out to make you the way you are . . . I don't think anything could ever melt you down.'

'No,' he agreed, but as he spoke he touched a hand to his scars; there were more, Sir Arthur Brake had told Glenda. Mal had also been severely burned about the shoulders.

A tremor seized hold of Glenda as she envisioned the look of him beneath the immaculate white suit and the white shirt that intensified the brazen tan of his skin. She glimpsed in him a Latin sensuality blended with the hardness; desires running hot and strong through the flesh and bone of his powerful body.

It wasn't only the demands of the foundry which had kept him away from Barton-le-Cross. There would have been women in his life who made his memory of a schoolgirl seem like milk compared to red wine.

'I don't intend to be cheated.' His gaze was fixed upon her white face as he spoke, then his eyes raked over her hair that was like a cap of flame. 'I want the d'Ath name carried on both in connection with the foundry and with the Château now at last it's mine.

Now, my dear, go to your *toilette* and then we'll dine and drink to the future.'

He extended a hand to her and drew her to her feet. In height she came only to his chin, though she wasn't a small girl. She felt the hard encirclement of his arm as he pressed her body to his and as she endured his closeness all she could think of was that despite his belief in her invention of a weak heart, it didn't swerve him from his purpose.

He didn't intend to change his plans; she felt it in the less than gentle way that he held her against him. His attitude sent a shudder right through her body and she made no attempt to suppress it; she wanted him to know that she disliked him touching her.

His fingers gripped her chin and he forced her face up to his so he could look down into her amber eyes, shaded by lashes and brows deeper in colour than her hair. Glenda wasn't pretty in the accepted sense; she had the fey quality often found in girls from the wild and mysterious valleys of Wales.

'I'm damned if I'll have you afraid of me,' he said. 'I want no coward for a son.'

'I'm not afraid of you,' she denied, fighting not to flinch at his words. 'I wouldn't give you that satisfaction.'

'No, there are other kinds of satisfaction I'd prefer from you.' Abruptly he lowered his head and his lips fastened upon hers, wringing from her a cry that was lost in the savage insistence of his kiss. It was as if a dark wave of bone and muscle swept over her, a force too strong for her to fight, so that she had to go swirling down into the depths of that kiss, laid back against his arm and panting through parted lips when at last he raised his head. Mal watched her through flickering black lashes, then he pushed her away from him and gestured towards a spiral stairway that seemed to lead to rooms above this large lounging area.

'Go and prepare yourself for dinner,' he ordered. 'And put some blusher on your cheeks, I don't want to sit looking at a ghost!'

'I'll make myself into a tart,' she flung over her shoulder as she went up the stairs. 'If that's the type of woman you're used to.'

The first thing Glenda noticed when she entered her bedroom was that her filmy apricot nightdress had been laid across the bed next to dark silk pyjamas.

She stood there upon the panel-chintz carpet, staring at that marriage of black and apricot silk. Images danced through her mind, and she was still acutely aware of how helpless she had been when Mal had chosen to make her so, giving her a taste of the passion men could feel without any need to love what they kissed and touched and took to bed.

'You don't happen to mean half as much to me as the getting of a son,' Mal had said.

She should have known . . . she should have guessed that a man who didn't bother to visit the girl he was engaged to was a man who had ordered a certain product and was satisfied that it would be delivered to him on the date it was due.

That product was herself. That was all she was to Malraux d'Ath. Her feelings and emotions didn't matter to him in the slightest; it probably hadn't occurred to him that she might care for another man.

CHAPTER THREE

GLENDA was still standing there bemused when a girl in a fawn dress and a cap came out of the bathroom, where there was a sound of running water.

'I have unpacked for Madame.' The girl shyly smiled but couldn't quite keep the eager curiosity out of her dark eyes. 'What evening dress and lingerie should I lay out?'

Like a genie the girl had seemed to appear by magic. 'I—is there another entrance to the tower?' Glenda asked, and she knew what lay in the back of her mind.

'From the rear, *madame*.'

'I see.' Glenda could feel her mind racing with possibilities; there was a way out if she dared to take it. She didn't have to stay here with a man she neither loved nor trusted. Oh, what a fool she had been in the first place to go through with a marriage with about as much sentiment attached to it as a prison sentence!

'What is your name?' she asked the maidservant.

'Fleur, *madame*.' The girl studied Glenda with a perplexed look; it was obvious that she expected a bride to look pleased with herself and only too ready to discuss a *toilette* that would dazzle the bridegroom.

'You have a pretty name, Fleur.' Glenda glanced around the bedroom and saw there was a door connecting it to another room. 'What is through there?'

'The room of Monsieur.' The girl blushed slightly and her gaze strayed to the fourposter upon which she

37

had arranged Glenda's nightdress and Mal's pyjamas.
'I took it for granted, *madame*——'

'Of course you did,' Glenda quickly reassured her.
'Fleur, I have a headache and would prefer to be alone
for a while. I'll lay out my dress myself and have a
bath—I don't need you right now, so run along.'

Fleur hesitated. 'Has Madame an aspirin?'

'Y-yes, of course. I'll manage—it's just that I want
to be alone for now. Today has been filled with people,
you understand?'

It was obvious that the girl didn't; that her young
mind was filled with romantic ideas about wedding
nights. With obvious reluctance she left the room,
departing through a door adjacent to the bathroom. As
the door closed behind her young figure, Glenda sank
down on a hassock and buried her face in her hands.
She was trembling with nerves, but had to brave herself for one of two things—either she stayed here and
made the best of a situation she was half responsible
for, or she left the Château by that rear exit in the
tower and tried to find a lodging for the night. There
had to be an *auberge* in that village they had passed
through on the way to the Château, and she was less
afraid of walking alone in the dark countryside than of
being trapped here like a rabbit in a snare.

She rose to her feet, took several steadying breaths,
then went across to the door through which Fleur had
vanished. She opened it to find a wall light illuminating
a narrow flight of stairs; they twisted and turned as
she hurried down them to where another of the wall
lights revealed a plain wooden door with an iron latch.

Glenda lifted the latch and stepped out into the cool
darkness . . . and the abrupt imprisonment of a pair of
frighteningly strong arms.

'I knew you'd try it on, my girl!'

As Mal swung her around to face him, her heart gave an erratic throb and a scream choked in her throat. It hadn't occurred to her that Mal would guess her intention and she had never suffered such a fright. 'Damn you——!' she panted.

'No doubt.' His hands bit into her waist and she felt the violence in his grip, and her own frustration as she struggled with him.

'Take your hands off me—you're insufferable!'

'And you're a fool.' Then as if he didn't care if he broke her backbone he bent her backwards and silenced her mouth with his . . . his lips were hard and hot with his anger and he kissed her until she was sobbing for breath. When he raised his head he still held her locked to him. 'Don't have a heart attack, will you?' he mocked.

'Oh, if I'd only known——'

'What, my dear?'

'What a brute you are.'

'Because I won't let you run out on me? The time to do so was in church this morning—I'd have understood that, but you stood there demurely and reciprocated the vows that made us man and wife. You said nothing, made no move when asked if we shouldn't be joined together. I could see your eyes through that veil and they made me think of a cornered vixen, but you went on with your responses, and when asked if you took me for your wedded husband, you said yes. When I took hold of your hand to put the ring on it, it was like ice, and I knew why you kept your veil over your eyes—it made my face less shocking to you. You were a romantic schoolgirl when we became engaged and when Grandpère asked you if you liked me, you whispered in his ear that you thought I looked ever so chivalrous. It highly amused him, and he repeated to me what you had said to him. "The girl takes you for her shining young *chevalier*, my boy. You had better not disappoint her." '

Mal's fingers bit bruisingly into Glenda's flesh. 'So sorry that you're disappointed in me, *ma chérie*, but I might say the same of you. You aren't quite the ardent young thing I remember, are you?'

Glenda hung there in his arms, and now—now was the moment for her to tell him the truth, except that the truth could only blacken Edith Hartwell's memory and reveal her as a woman who had tricked money out of the Malraux family. Glenda couldn't do it; she bit back the words that might have helped Mal to understand her behaviour. Oh, better to let him believe that she couldn't stand the look of him ... husband he might be, but he was a stranger as well.

Edith ... dear, impulsive, extravagant Edith had taken a foundling to her heart and a very real affection had grown up between them. Nothing could spoil for Glenda the memory of Edith the first time they met, such a contrast in her warm furs to the bleak-faced Principal of the foundling home.

'Oh, those poor thin legs!' Edith had exclaimed. 'You need fattening up, child.' And then and there she had carried Glenda off to the best restaurant in town and stuffed her with roast chicken, chocolate ice-cream, and fondants wrapped in foil. Edith didn't eat well herself, but she had loved champagne and she had sat there sipping her Bollinger and seeming in a young orphan's eyes like the Fairy Godmother who came and swept Cinderella out of the kitchen.

Betrayal of that love wasn't in Glenda, so she kept

her mouth shut and accepted from Mal his scorn and anger.

'To hell with what you think of my ruin of a face!' The words cut into Glenda with the cruelty of a rip-hook. 'You're no different from all other women . . . in all of them there is *l'amour fou*.'

Wild love, she thought. Her eyes burned in her white face as she looked away from Mal, looked across the courtyard to the tall iron gates that were now shut for the night.

'It's no good looking like that.' Mal gave her a shake. 'You can't get away from me, anyway. All this land hereabouts is mine, *à perte de vue!* As far as your eyes can see!'

His *domaine de droit*, she thought, as she was his whether or not he wanted her.

'We shall now return to our apartment, and this time you will do as you are told.' He turned her to the stairs and half-pushed her all the way to the top, and then in through the door of the bedroom. She didn't dare to think what his intentions might be as he gave her another push that sent her staggering in the direction of the great bed spread with old French lace and their articles of nightwear.

'Don't vex me any more tonight,' he threatened. 'You'll bathe yourself, and then you'll put on a dress suitable for a wedding supper. Do you hear me?'

'I would have to be stone deaf not to,' she retorted.

'Has the girl unpacked for you?' He swept his eyes around the room, which was handsomely furnished with an oyster-shell bureau and matching vanity-table, several armchairs upholstered in a thick silk that matched the window curtains, and a pair of *armoires*

set into angles of the room, whose dominating feature
was the bed.

Mal strode across and took a look in the *armoires*,
one of which now held Glenda's clothing. He raked a
hand through the dresses and there was a whisper of
satin as he made his selection and showed it to Glenda,
honey-gold with a long flowing skirt.

'Wear this,' he ordered. 'And buck yourself up, or
we'll be eating our wedding supper for breakfast.'

She made no protest and after watching her a
moment through narrowed eyes he entered his own
room, pausing just a moment to add: 'I've my own
shower in here, so you may have full use of the bathroom . . . it perhaps wouldn't be good for your nerves
if I suggested sharing it before we become better
acquainted. When did those nerves of yours take a turn
for the worst? You had plenty of cheek when you were
a child!'

The door closed with a click behind him and Glenda
stared across the room as if his tall dark image was
imprinted in the wood. It seemed there was no way
out of the trap she was in; the iron gates were closed
and they were so immense that she doubted if she could
open them. She suspected that if she got them open, they
would be fitted with an alarm device in case of intruders.
It was evident from this room alone that the Château had
things in it that would be well worth stealing.

Glenda kicked off her shoes and felt the thickness of
the chintz-panel carpet as she went to the bureau, attracted by a Columbine figure companioned by
Harlequin. They were made of porcelain and their
detail and colouring were so perfect that they had to
be Dresden. She picked up Columbine very carefully
and examined the base; it was Edith who had taught

her to have an eye for things of artistic merit, just as she had taught her to appreciate good music, fine acting, and the dissection of the human heart in the writings of Henry James. Glenda remembered with a slight smile how she had protested at all the long words and the involved sentences.

'Nothing that is easy of enjoyment is of much use,' Edith had said. 'And just think of all the long words you'll know by the time you've read the works of Mr James!'

So Glenda had obligingly read those puzzling, involved, yet strangely fascinating novels and stories. In her ten years with Edith she had rarely refused to do as she was told, but she wondered as she studied Harlequin if she would have refused to marry Mal had Edith lived.

Suddenly the small carriage clock on the bureau began to chime and she looked at it startled. Eight o'clock, and she still wasn't ready for dinner!

Hastily she went into the bathroom, shed her clothes and stepped into the tepid bath which twenty minutes ago had been a hot one. She quickly bathed, just as quickly dried herself and flung talcum-powder on her damp patches. It wasn't that she was scared of Mal, she assured herself; she just didn't want him to come fuming into the bedroom before she had her undies on.

But it happened! She was raking about in the drawer for the slip and panties that matched the honey-gold dress when Mal strode in, resplendent himself in a matt-black dinner suit.

'*Je suis enchanté!*' he said, as she swung round with a silk slip clutched to her.

'I—I'm not dressed!'

'I can see that, *chérie*.' His eyes raked her from head to toe. 'I chose a fortunate moment, eh?'

'P-please leave me to get ready——' She pressed the flimsy slip closer to her as she met his eyes and saw how he was looking at her. 'I—I shan't be very much longer——'

'*Ma chérie*, I'm not so sure that I want you covered up.' A long stride brought him to her and she shrank away as he reached for her.

'No, Mal!' It was a half-scream as his hands closed upon her bare body.

His hands stroked up her sides, and then he plucked away the slip and threw it to the carpet. Uncaring of her feelings, he gathered her soft and shapely whiteness to him, and one of his hands slid down to the small of her back.

'*Dieu*, what skin you have! It's like touching a baby, and in some ways you're as innocent as a baby, aren't you? Come, relax, let happen what must happen——'

'*No!*' Like a mad thing she fought and kicked, but Mal only laughed at her ineffectual efforts to get out of his arms.

'Yes, *ma chère*, there will never be a more propitious moment than this, you must admit it.'

She flung him a beseeching look and caught amusement in his eyes . . . was he teasing her?

'What a child you are, Glenda!'

'Am I?'

'In some ways.' His amused eyes strayed over her. 'Men have various hungers, *mignonne*, but right now mine is for a square meal and several glasses of wine, enticing as you are. *Bien sûr*, but this skin of yours is quite incredibly white and makes mine look like an Arab's. *Rose-white youth, passionate pale . . . Oh, there's nothing in life so finely frail as rose-white youth."* '

'If we're going to eat, Mal, then I have to get dressed——' He confused her with his quotation, and she'd feel safer out of his arms. 'Oh, look at the time!'

'So you have to get dressed?'

'Of course.'

He laughed, as if to himself. 'Spare me the coy virgin, yet if you were not that, then I'd want to know why not.'

'Men are such——' She caught her breath, for her heart was beating so fast. 'They take such a chauvinistic view of life where women are concerned, yet none of you are saints! You start seducing every female in sight the moment you're able to, yet you still expect to marry a girl who hasn't been seduced.'

'A man expects discretion of a fiancée, *ma belle*. Now may I assist you to dress, if dress you must?'

'No, you may not!'

'Then you are going to stay as you are?'

'Stop it, Mal, and go away while I get dressed.'

'I want to stay and watch you.'

'No——'

'I'm your husband and I have my rights.'

'You're doing your best to—to embarrass me,' she accused.

'You have to stop being embarrassed by me.' He dropped a kiss into the hollow of her shoulder, then let her out of his arms. He walked to one of the armchairs and sprawled down in it, stretching his long legs across the carpet. 'This is the first time I've had a wife and I want to watch you get dressed, Glenda. You might as well make a start, or we'll be here all night.'

'What an obstinate devil you are!' She snatched up her slip and felt the rosy warming of her skin as he watched her put it on. She had to pass him in order to get her panties from the drawer, and then came the ordeal of stepping into them.

'You—you're making me feel like a tart!' she burst out. 'I begin to think that you're quite sadistic.'

'Nonsense, my dear. A woman looks charming when she steps into her smalls, but a man's so clumsy when he steps into his.'

'I hope I'm not to be treated to *that* performance!' She took her dress from its hanger and slid the whispering satin down over her head; she heard Mal laugh softly as he came and stood behind her, his fingers closing the zip. He turned her to face him and his eyes appraised her from head to toe. 'Your mother taught you good taste, didn't she?'

'She did her best,' Glenda admitted. She could feel Mal watching her through the black lashes that made his eyes glitter. 'I have to put on my shoes——'

'I'm not stopping you.'

'N-no, of course not.' She turned to the *armoire* and fumbled about for her satin slippers; she dropped one and Mal picked it up, quirking an eyebrow at its slim elegance.

'Come, Cinderella, be seated while your less than handsome prince helps you on with your slippers.'

She was learning that he wasn't to be argued with, so she sat down on the dressing-stool and watched his dark head as he slid her feet into her slippers. Then he glanced up at her, too quickly for her to conceal what came into her eyes as the vanity-table lamps lit the cruel ravagement down one side of his face. His eyes locked with hers, capturing her look of recoil.

'Perhaps I should get myself a black satin mask, eh?'

There was in his words a kind of poignancy, and

Glenda wished she could bring herself to touch his face and perhaps ease the hurt he must feel each time some stranger in the street, some diner in a restaurant, some graceless little fool like herself told him with a look that he was forbidding.

'Being in a fire must be a nightmare,' she said. 'It must haunt your dreams sometimes?'

'It does,' he said curtly, and rose to his feet. He stood there looking into the mirror at his face, then he turned away. 'I'm sorry, Glenda, that you have a Caliban for a husband instead of a *preux chevalier*.'

'Mal——'

But even as she spoke his name, the door was closing behind him, and Glenda turned slowly to face her own face in the mirror. She had always been sensitive to other people's pain and had she and Malraux d'Ath been friends instead of two people who were married for all the wrong reasons she would have found it easier to show her compassion.

She stroked a hand down her own cheek and tried to imagine what it must be like to feel the ridges of burn scars ... first degree burns, which must have been so bad at the time that there had been little chance of saving his looks; the important thing had been to save his life. It was possible that a long course of facial surgery might lessen the ravages, but the removal of scars only left other scars, and she doubted if Mal had the patience or the vanity to undergo the operations. He had, in fact, said as much, as if warning her that she might as well get used to the look of him because he had more important things to do than to cater to the wishes of a wife he didn't happen to be in love with.

She sighed and ran a comb through her hair, styled to the heart shape of her face. She never used a lot of make-up, so it didn't take long to apply feather-finish to her face and the coral-rose lipstick that outlined her mouth, the full lower lip indented right at the centre.

As she studied her reflection words drifted into her mind and a smile played about her lips. 'They call your type of mouth bee-stung,' Simon Brake had told her, that weekend he was on leave from the Guards and had escorted Edith and herself to the latest production of *The King and I*. She had been seventeen at the time and all at once aware of the charm and good looks of Sir Arthur's Guardsman son. She had noticed in the foyer of the theatre the glances he attracted from women, but he had seemed not to notice as he gave his attention to Edith and herself. He had bought her a box of chocolates, and afterwards she had kept her programme and wrote in it that Yul Brynner was a marvellous actor, and that Simon Brake was every bit as attractive... and he had paid her a compliment.

Into her reflections came the chiming of the little carriage-clock here in this rotunda of a bedroom, quite a distance from Chelsea where Captain Simon Brake had his rooms.

She rose from the dressing-stool and smoothed the skirt of her dress. Her neck looked rather bare, for the dress had a rather low-cut *décolleté*, and after a moment of hesitation she added the lovely *croix d'or* she had worn that morning with her wedding dress.

It glimmered there in her neckline, and she thought of the superstition attached to the cross, that it was supposed to guard the wearer from the demons of the night.

A draught from somewhere, perhaps from an open window, ran its touch over her skin and all at once she was hurrying to the door, her skirt held above her slippers as she made her way down the twisting stairs that led to the lower room, where candles were lit upon a table set for two, and where a great log fire was glowing.

The room looked warm and inviting, and the food waited on a side table beneath silver warmers. Glenda closed the door behind her and her satin dress whispered as she moved towards the fire. Mal was pulling the cork of a long-necked bottle and the candle flames cast his shadow darkly up the white walls and across the ceiling so that he seemed to loom over her.

'No rouge, I see.' The cork hissed and there was a spill of wine down the bottle as he filled a pair of cut glass bowls on fluted stems.

'I'm sorry if you're disappointed,' she rejoined, 'but I never wear rouge and wouldn't know how to apply it.'

'I'm not disappointed, my dear. You look too charming for words.' As he invited her to take one of the wine bowls, his eyes dwelt on the *croix d'or* in the neck of her dress. 'That's very nice; I noticed you were wearing it in church this morning.'

'I was given it as a wedding present.' She cupped her wine bowl in her quivering hands . . . each time she was with Mal she felt a nervous tension that made every glance and gesture seem extra significant; the words they parried seemed like the cut and thrust of foils.

'From whom?'

'A—friend.'

'Someone known to me?'

'Hardly, when you've never been to Barton-le-Cross.'

'That seems to rankle with you, Glenda, that I never came courting you.'

'We should have got better acquainted,' she told him.

'Perhaps so, but I had a business to run, and then there was the fire and my face took time to heal. In any case,' he shrugged, 'our marriage was a foregone conclusion.'

'Was it really, Mal?'

His eyes narrowed into slits of steel. 'We are here together at the Château to prove it, *ma chère*. As I was saying, the golden cross becomes you, but brides are usually presented with pots and pans and teamakers. Who was the giver?'

'Sir Arthur Brake's son.' There, she had said it calmly enough and it didn't show that under the honey-gold satin and the slight weight of the cross her heart was racing. 'Sir Arthur was a long-standing friend of Edith's, so I naturally met his son.'

'Naturally.' Mal raised his wine bowl and studied the glimmer of the wine through the crystal facets. 'Why shouldn't you wear his *gage d'amour* at your wedding to me?'

'It isn't a love token,' she protested.

'Then has it some other significance for you, *petite*? You know, in the deep heart of France there are those who cross themselves when the shadows fall and the Loire river glimmers with the sheen of black pearls. "*What was he doing, the great god Pan, Down in the reeds by the river?*" '

Glenda shivered as she met Mal's eyes, whose steel had been tempered in a fire which had left him as sinister as the demon-god whom Elizabeth Barrett Browning had described with such fluent strokes of the pen.

'You know that poem?' Mal asked.

'Yes.'

'She had a significant way with words, eh? Come, we must drink to each other.' Mal stepped closer to her and tapped the rim of his wine bowl to hers so they chimed in unison. '*Bonheur!*'

Happiness? Could she really believe that such a thing was possible when she had left the eager longings of her heart in the hands of another man? There was no way to stop herself from contrasting the way Mal made her feel to the way she had felt in Simon's company. He had hung the cross around her neck and his eyes had looked right into hers. 'Wear this and I'll know you're thinking of me even as you marry him! Had Shakespeare been the author of our story, then I'd be killing you instead of letting you go through with such a damnable arrangement!'

Emotion rose in her throat and in order to try and ease the pain she gulped her wine.

'You don't,' Mal exclaimed, 'treat Montrachet like Coca-Cola!'

'M-my throat's dry——'

'And there's a little hint of tears, *non?* It was a sadness for you that your mother couldn't be with you at the wedding, but you had your friends, Sir Arthur and his son.'

Glenda shot a look at Mal, but his face was masked in politeness and only the twisted edge of his lip showed her that he was being sardonic.

'Let us eat,' he said decisively. 'I'm quite ravenous myself.'

To start the meal they had truffles seasoned and creamed, and as Glenda forked some of the delicious mixture into her mouth, Mal watched her from across the table. 'There is a belief that truffles were the food of emperors; sensual food that is supposed to make women more tender and men more passionate.'

'Is that why we're having it?' she asked, though she could hardly bear to think of his passion in relation to herself. Knowing she didn't love him, he would treat her as if he had bought her in the market place . . . and in a sense he had, for she settled the Malraux account which Edith Hartwell had drawn on for years, sharing those benefits with Glenda herself. Malraux money had educated her and sent her to good schools, it had provided her with nice clothes, trips abroad, and parties in the debutante tradition. Edith had insisted on that. She had said that it was the accepted mode among those of the upper middle classes of which she was a member, and of which Glenda had become a member when she became her adopted daughter.

It had all been very pleasant, but always in Glenda's mind had lurked the knowledge that the pleasantries of life had a price-tag attached to them . . . when she had finally learned from Edith what the price amounted to, she had wanted to resist, to rebel, even to run away, for by then she had felt her heart's excitement whenever the telephone rang and it was Simon saying he had time off from his duties and would she like to take in a matinee, go to tea at the Ritz, or drive into the country. For during that debutante season Edith had insisted upon, they had taken a flat in London. Then Edith had realised that she was becoming attached to Simon, so they had gone home to Barton-le-Cross. 'You have to remember that you're engaged to someone else,' Edith had said, gently enough. 'I know how attractive Simon is, especially in his uniform, but the Brakes aren't all that well off, you know. Simon has only his pay.'

Glenda ate her meat garnished with *coeur d'arti-chaut*, for she was hungry but without the interest to appreciate the flavour of the food, which was very French and therefore excellent.

Where, she wondered, would she be right now if Edith Hartwell had not visited that orphanage at Llandudno? How different her life would have been. Very likely she would have become a typist in an office, or a factory worker.

There would have been no dances at Claridges, no cream teas at the Ritz in the company of a dashing officer in the Guards.

Nor would there have been her marriage to a man she neither loved nor particularly admired.

There he sits, she thought, the man she had married even as the man she longed for had stood in the church and watched her become the bride of the lean, half-French, scar-faced Malraux d'Ath.

Had she secretly hoped that when the Rector asked if there was any impediment to the marriage, Simon would have stepped forward and announced to everyone that she belonged to him?

Glenda had thought of herself as belonging to Simon ever since that night in York . . . that tremendous night when the lightning had clashed across the skies and the thunder, so Simon declared, sounded as if the Charge of the Light Brigade was taking place on the Yorkshire moors.

Tears of longing . . . tears of regret trembled in her eyes as she reached for her wine and drank Montrachet salted by teardrops she couldn't hold back. She was glad that Mal had his back to her, for he was at the side table and about to perform a feat taught him by a friend who was in the restaurant business.

'It was soon after my accident,' the words drifted over his shoulder. 'Raf realised that if I didn't face up to what had hurt me, then I'd be a nerve case. So he did a very simple thing and it worked—he taught me the fascinating art of making *crêpes Suzette. Voilà!*'

Mal turned with the flaming pan in his hand and there was a tang of oranges and cognac as the *crêpes Suzette* curled and cooked among the blue-tinged flames. Flames that leapt and cast their sorcerous light over the scarred face as Mal bent over Glenda and placed the delicacy on her plate.

She looked at him and saw the flames reflected in his eyes. 'There, if the foundry ever fails,' he said, 'I can become a waiter.'

'I don't see you as a waiter,' she rejoined.

'How do you see me, Glenda?'

She wanted to tell him he was a dark shadow which had eclipsed those sunlit, stolen hours she had shared with Simon Brake.

The misery of being here with Mal when she wanted to be with Simon washed over her. Why had Simon stood by and let her marry Mal? How could he have done that after telling her that he loved her?

'Eat your *crêpe* while it is still hot,' Mal urged.

She took up her fork and obeyed him. 'What's the verdict?' he asked.

'Delicious,' she murmured.

'You said that as if it tasted of nothing.'

'Well, what am I supposed to say?' The resentment in her eyes was shaded by her lashes. 'Am I supposed to jump for joy?'

'Don't be childish——'

'Childish, am I, just because I can't swoon over a pancake!'

'Thank you, my dear, for the enthusiasm.' Abruptly he looped a finger in the chain of her cross. 'I haven't said a lot about this, but I don't want you to wear it again.'

'I—I'll wear it whenever I please!'

'No, Glenda, not if I tell you not to.'

'I won't be bullied——'

'I don't intend to bully you, but I do intend to have a wife who belongs to me and isn't sentimentally attached by a cross and chain to someone else. Understood?'

She moistened dry lips with the tip of her tongue. 'It's a present and I happen to like it—wives these days can't be ordered about and told what to do. The Dark Ages are over!'

Their eyes locked, and then he gave that soft laughter that seemed to begin and end deep in his throat. 'You have quite a temper to go with that hair, haven't you? You're quite a little vixen on the quiet, with some fire in you. I wonder if I'm glad that you didn't grow up to be the eager little chatterbox I expected, who might want to put cretonne covers on the couches and bake currant cakes for my tea.'

'Is there so much difference between currant cakes and *crêpes Suzette*?' Glenda asked.

She heard the intake of his breath, then the rattle of the pan on the side table. 'You were a sweet child, or is my memory playing tricks?'

Glenda felt the beating of her heart . . . what if she told him, blurted out that she had never been inside this house before today, and hadn't known of his existence until she was a teenager? What would be his reaction . . . would he apply for an annulment of the marriage?

As she watched him with wide and questioning eyes he came back to where she sat, his darkness filling her vision until everything else was blotted out.

'Sweet or not,' he murmured, 'you are mine, *petite sorcière*.'

'Mal, I'm not——'

He didn't let her finish, he placed a finger over her lips. 'Don't persist in arguing with me, *mignonne*. In some beauty there is a strangeness, an enchantment in the way skin, hair and bone structure catch the light and shadow. You have this quality, Glenda, and it's something I should like passed on to a child of ours.'

'Mal, please listen to me——'

'Be silent.' And this time he stopped her words with his lips, lifting her from her chair until he was able to sweep her up into his arms, and his lips held hers as he pinched out the candle flames and by the light of the wall-lamps carried her up the stairs to the *chambre à coucher*.

CHAPTER FOUR

MAL stood with her there beside the bed with its four tall posts rising to the ceiling, and all she could think of was that she wouldn't be made love to by a man who didn't love her. She wouldn't tamely submit to him, not without a fight.

She looked up into Mal's eyes and saw the passion darkening them. 'There's something you don't know—you must listen to me!'

'This is no time for talking, *chérie*.' His fingers were feeling for the zip of her dress and as he began to peel open her dress and she felt the satin falling away from her shoulders, she cried out, like some incantation against the devil:

'You could never be sure if it was your child!'

'What do you say?' His voice was blurred against her skin as he kissed the soft white curve of her shoulders.

'I—I've been with Simon.'

Mal's lips stopped their caressing movements and his eyes slid like hot steel over her face. 'You will say that again!'

'I've slept with Simon Brake.' The words came with a rush, and some of what she was going to say was true.

'You had better be lying to me, Glenda.' Mal's fingers bit into her flesh and his face darkened so his scars looked livid and ugly.

57

'You might have guessed,' she said recklessly. 'He's too good-looking for a girl to be able to—to say no to him.' Those words about Simon's good looks hung between Glenda and this man whose face had been ravaged by fire. With deliberate intent she let her eyes rest on his scars as she went on:

'I've known and loved Simon for a long time. Edith—my mother never knew the way I felt about him because it would have upset her, but after she died—we just couldn't help ourselves——'

'And when did your overwhelming feelings for each other reach their rapturous conclusion, eh?' Mal's voice was low but charged with sarcasm, and his fingers had slid up from her shoulders and were pressing the sides of her neck.

'Simon's father has a house at York a-and after my mother died I went up there to spend a few days. It happened—the way these things do.'

'You were carried away by your emotions, is that it, and by the good looks of the dashing Guardsman? How romantic!'

'It was,' she asserted. And there was just enough shaken emotion in her voice to make her sound convincing. She *had* spent a night all alone with Simon—he had suggested that they go riding on the moors because the fresh air would do her good and help clear her mind of the belief everyone has when someone beloved dies, that they could have done something to hold death at bay.

Then, as if the drama of that sorrowful week had to be played out to the full, she and Simon had ridden into one of the worst storms to hit York for a long time. They had taken shelter in a tumbledown old cottage on the moors, quite untenanted except for fieldmice and spiders, and it had kept on raining . . . raining as if the skies had been split open by the lightning.

There had been no hope of getting home until the storm abated, so Simon had brought the horses into the cottage out of the teeming rain and the bright glare of the lightning which might have caused them to bolt off. He had lit a fire in the old grate of the cottage parlour and they had huddled together and feasted on a couple of candy bars. When she grew sleepy Simon had urged her to relax and sleep; he'd wake her when the storm went over.

They had finally arrived home at four o'clock in the morning, finding dead birds and broken flowers on the bridle path. Before going into the house Simon had taken her into his arms and kissed her; it was then he had told her that he thought they were in love.

'So you're telling me that Simon Brake has been your lover?' Mal's words broke in upon her thoughts.

'Yes,' she said simply. What was one more lie among all the lies she had lived through today? This lie had the ring of truth . . . perhaps she and Simon might have made love had they not been aware of Edith's ghost haunting that old cottage.

'You little tramp!' Mal swung his hand, but even as Glenda stood and defied him and waited for the blow to connect with her face, he slowly drew back his hand until it came to rest against his own cheek, the fingers spreading as if to shield his scars. Glenda watched him in a palpitating silence . . . in fear of him but exultant because she had convinced him that Simon had possessed her before he exerted his unloving rights; before he used her in order to get a child from her, preferably a boy to be trained for the foundry as he had been trained by Duval Malraux.

'As you say,' Mal spoke sombrely, 'I'd never be sure if the child was mine.'

Something twisted inside Glenda, for never before in her life had she been cruel to a living thing. She hated cruelty, but she had to defend what she felt for Simon; she couldn't rid her mind of his image, nor the kiss they had shared as dawn broke over the wet moorland. 'I feel that you belong to me,' he had said. 'That nothing should come between us.'

'Mal,' she pleaded, 'let me go. Have our marriage annulled.'

'I think not.' His eyes swept her up and down contemptuously. 'I'm not handing you over to your handsome lover, you are going to stay here at the Château Noir with your ugly husband. People will point us out to each other; we'll be Beauty and the Beast, and I'll put you through hell for telling me about yourself and the gallant Guardsman.'

He walked to the door, and Glenda watched him guardedly. Perhaps he wouldn't touch her but satisfy himself by calling her names and saying bitter things.

Such a hope was shortlived; there was a click as he turned the key in the lock and then came deliberately back to where she stood. There was malevolence in his eyes as he studied the dawning look of horror in her eyes.

'There's one thing to be said for shopsoiled goods.' Mal reached for her, and his grip was bruising. 'I shan't have to take too much care about handling you, shall I?'

He took the neck of her dress in his hand and ripped it downwards as if it had been paper. Piece by piece her clothing was torn from her and scattered, and he didn't seem to care, or even to feel the scratches which she inflicted upon him in the desperate, uneven battle. 'Rapist!' she screamed, as he flung her on the bed—a scream that would have penetrated walls less solid than those of the stone tower. She thrashed and clawed and dredged up from the past some of the bad language learned at the orphanage where children of all kinds had been mixed up together. She was maddened as a creature in a trap who bites through its own flesh and bone in an effort to get free.

'You look as if I'd got you on the rack.' Mal held her beneath him and seemed to enjoy her struggles. 'What a profane little tongue you have, my dear! What did you think when we stood at the altar this morning, that I intended to treat you like some holy vessel? That all you had to say to me was sorry but you fancied some other man and would I please keep my hands to myself? If it wasn't for your colourful language, *petite*, I'd find your innocence quite remarkable. No wonder the gallant Captain Brake found you easy to seduce!'

'Simon isn't like you,' she glared up at Mal, flexing the fingernails of her pinioned hands, 'he isn't a brute without feelings.'

'Rest assured that I have feelings, Glenda, and you'll share them, *ma belle*. You'll share them up to the hilt!'

'I'd sooner be dead!' He still hadn't defeated her, and if all she could do was to hurt him with words, then she found them and threw them in his face.

'Your scars sicken me, Mal. If you must use me, then do you mind turning out the light so I don't have to look at you?'

There was a deadly hush and the blood seemed to drain away from under his tanned skin, leaving behind the shocking lividity of his scars. He had gone animal-still except for his eyes, which seethed with a rage so molten that Glenda involuntarily closed her eyes and waited for the pain of being struck . . . or choked.

'*Dieu*, but you have the tongue of a bitch!' He released her, letting go of her as if suddenly she was repellent to him. He slid from the bed and left her lying in the crucified position in which he had held her, her dark flame of hair pillowing her defiant face.

Her eyelids flickered and through her lashes she saw him standing at the bedside, big and dark against the lamplight, his face shadowed except for the glitter of his eyes. 'Why did you marry me?' As he asked the question his eyes went over her body with the edge of hardened steel. 'Do the Brakes happen to be impoverished?'

'It was Edith's—my mother's dying wish.' Glenda caught at the lace coverlet and drew it over her nudity; she couldn't endure that look Mal was giving her . . . no longer a sensual look but a steel-cold one whose very edge she seemed to feel.

'How very moving,' he jibed. 'Naturally it wouldn't have anything to do with money?'

'We're not all mercenary——'

'Edith—your mother—was generously looked after in my grandfather's will.'

'I know——' Glenda bit her lip, feeling there the throb of a nerve. 'And you got what you wanted—the Château.'

'While poor little Glenda got torn from the arms of her gallant soldier boy, who stood in that church this morning and watched you become my wife. I swear if I loved a girl I couldn't do that! I'd either snatch her from the altar steps, or take myself off to Timbuctoo. But of course, it takes all sorts to make fools of women.'

He turned away from the bed and went towards the door he had locked. 'I won't stay to disturb your dreams,' he threw over his shoulder. 'I wouldn't want to give you a nightmare.'

The door closed behind him and there was silence in the bedroom. Glenda could hardly believe that she was alone, and for several minutes her heart still throbbed with apprehension. Then in a while her nostrils tensed to the drifting aroma of a cigar and she knew that Mal was out on the balcony of his room and the night air was wafting the smoke in through her open windows.

Oh God—she turned in the cocoon of the coverlet and pressed her face into the pillows. Every now and then a tremor still shook her body . . . she had never hurt any living thing the way she had hurt Mal tonight, and she felt sure she would remember that bitter, burning look in his eyes until the day she died.

For a long time the cigar smoke drifted in, and Glenda lay there sleepless, her gaze upon the windows where the night beyond them was moonless, utterly drenched in darkness.

She didn't sleep until the pallor of dawn began to seep into the room. It wasn't until the birds started to sing that she closed her eyes and allowed her body to find some relaxation. She went off to sleep, and it was noon when the young maid Fleur came to wake her; there was a hint of a knowing smile in the girl's eyes, as if it was expected of a bride to sleep away the morning after her wedding night.

'Madame has had a good long rest,' Fleur smiled, pulling aside the long full curtains and letting a brilliant ray of sunshine into the room. 'Monsieur has gone out riding; he told me not to disturb you.'

Glenda sat up in bed, and then blushed as she realised that she wore no nightdress, and that her clothing from the evening before was scattered about the room.

Fleur picked up her torn evening dress and looked at it in some amazement. She glanced at Glenda, who was struggling into her robe. '*Madame,* look at what has happened to your dress!'

'I know, Fleur.' Glenda went to the vanity-table and picked up a comb and as she ran it through her hair, the thought ran through her mind that her maid was going to have quite a titbit of gossip to relate to the other maids. It would probably strike them as exciting that a husband should be in such a hurry to make love to his wife.

'Should I try and mend the dress, *madame?*'

Glenda shook her head. 'Throw it away, Fleur. I'd say it's damaged beyond repair.'

As her marriage was damaged . . . this marriage of duty on her part, and of gain on Mal's.

'Such lovely satin as well!' Fleur stroked a hand down the long skirt.

'There's probably enough there for you to make a shirt for yourself, Fleur.' Glenda turned from the mirror, smiling slightly. 'Are you good at dressmaking?'

'*Oui, madame.*' Fleur carefully folded the dress and placed it on a chair. 'Shall I run you a bath, *madame,* or will you take a shower?'

'I'll shower.' Glenda didn't think there was any point in asking Fleur not to mention how the dress came to be torn; the girl seemed to accept as perfectly natural the excess of passion which had caused the damage and she naturally assumed that the passion had been of a loving kind. No doubt the outcome of Glenda's actual wedding night would have astonished her.

After Glenda had showered she went to the *armoire* to select a dress for what would no doubt be a family luncheon. She dreaded it, but it had to be faced; later on today she would find an opportunity to speak alone with Mal regarding her return to England. She meant to return; he had what he wanted out of this awful marriage so he couldn't deny her what she wanted.

Thanks to Edith's generosity Glenda had some really nice clothes, and after due consideration she selected a dove-coloured dress with black pin-dots, simple but beautifully cut. A brisk combing settled her hair into shape and it took only a matter of minutes for her to apply her usual light make-up.

'Will I do, Fleur?' she asked, stroking the sides of her dress rather nervously. She had refused breakfast except for a cup of coffee, but knew it would be expected of her to partake of lunch.

'*Oui, madame*, you look *très chic*.'

'You speak very good English, Fleur—why is that?'

'Because Monsieur has always had English business people visiting the Château, and also relatives on his father's side. His widowed sister lives here with her son Robert, as you know.'

Glenda knew there was a sister by the name of Jeanne; a few years previously she had been badly hurt in the horrific accident which had killed her American husband. They had been on vacation in Florida and had been staying at one of the towering, newly built hotels serviced by express lifts. One evening one of the lifts had failed to function correctly and it had crashed into the basement of the hotel, killing most of the pas-

sengers and injuring two of them. Jeanne had survived
because her husband, who must have realised what was
going to happen, had held her in his arms and cushioned her with his body.

Jeanne had lived, according to Edith at the cost of
her nerves. For months after the accident she had been
a nervous wreck. What Glenda hadn't known was that
Jeanne Talbot lived at the Château Noir with her son,
who would be about seven years old.

Fleur handed Glenda her perfume, which was in the
black crystal atomizer which had belonged to Edith. It
still contained Arpège, which had been Edith's favourite perfume, and as Glenda lightly sprayed it on she
had a vivid image of the woman who had so influenced
her life. There had always been something of the
Thirties era about Edith Hartwell, in her sleek chignon
hairstyle, in the way she dressed, so simply and yet so
stylishly. Glenda didn't dare to think how much it had
cost the Malraux estate to sustain Edith's life style, the
provision being made because Duval Malraux had
taken such a fancy to her daughter.

Glenda gazed at her reflection in the vanity-table
mirror and saw there the cool, poised, ladylike person
Edith had taught her to be, all in order to fool Malraux
d'Ath. She turned away from the mirror and the twist
of distaste on her mouth was for herself . . . the bitter
things she had said to Mal had left their taste in her
mouth.

'You had better lead the way to the main part of the
house,' she said to Fleur. 'I'm bound to lose myself—I
had no idea the Château was so large.'

'But you came here when you were a child, did you
not, *madame*?'

'Oh, children forget things.' Glenda felt that nervous

skip of the heart that reminded her that she was living a lie and was entangled in a web of deception she just had to break out of. She glanced away when Fleur picked up the torn satin dress which was such a painful reminder of last night and the things she and Mal had said to each other. She didn't love him, but she hated to remember that ashen look of his when she had told him that she couldn't bear to look at him.

The hot sun of noon stroked the silver-grey walls of the Château as Fleur led her from the tower and across a paved court to an oval-shaped door that stood partly ajar. Above the door were stone carvings of gargoyles and beaked birds gazing down at Glenda with a kind of malevolence, and lost in a profusion of musty leaves were some stone letters which probably spelled out the motto of the original owner of the Château; no doubt something very arrogant and menacing.

Sunlight streamed through the gothic windows as Glenda entered the hall, lighting on the deep dower chests under the windows, on leather books in mullioned cases, and on armoured knights, helmeted heads bowed over broadswords.

Glenda glanced around the hall, above which were dark cross-beams hung with enormous chandeliers, and there was a central staircase of the same dark timber, the treads carpeted in cardinal red.

The effect was of time arrested, all signs of the modern world eliminated from this Château which hung as if enchanted upon weathered cliffs above the Loire, clinging like a fantasy of cowled towers and diamond-paned windows draped in ivy leaves which the sun struck to pieces of carved metal.

No wonder Malraux d'Ath had wanted it for his own

. . . no wonder he had thought a loveless marriage worth the price!

Except that Glenda couldn't tolerate it . . . Mal had to release her so she could go to Simon, free at last of her obligation to Edith Hartwell.

She gave a start when Fleur touched her arm. '*Madame*, that door over there leads into the *salon*. The family will be assembling there for luncheon.'

'Thank you, Fleur.' Bracing herself Glenda walked across the hall to the indicated door, oval-shaped like all the others with a kind of reddish gleam in the wood. She entered the *salon* and instantly the group of people there stopped talking and Glenda felt their eyes taking her in from head to toe. Her instinct was to turn and run away, but that would have been childish.

'There you are, *ma chère*.' The tall breeched figure of Mal detached himself from the group and as he came towards her, his eyes glittered coldly. 'I've been telling everyone that you felt like a lie in this morning. Are you now feeling rested, *chérie*?'

Glenda felt herself blushing even though his inference had so little truth in it; she looked up into his eyes and they were menacing and far from lover-like. But he had his back to his family as he greeted her, and when he bent his tall head to kiss her, it wasn't an endearment that he whispered.

'Don't you dare to let me down,' he muttered between his teeth, for her ears alone.

Holding her by the elbow, he led her towards his family, to whom she was to make believe that all was as it should be between a newly married man and his wife. It was the gall of the man that gave her a breathless, lost-for-words look. What was he up to? He must realise after the fiasco of last night that she couldn't stay under his roof to go on living a lie!

'*Ma chère*, let me introduce you to my Aunt Héloise, who was disappointed not to be at our wedding but who doesn't get about as much as she would like on account of a painful hip. Tante, this is Glenda.'

His aunt had a rather drawn face, as if she was often in pain, but her eyes were kindly enough. She was dressed extremely well in a dark dress with a beautiful lace collar which looked handmade. In the lobes of her ears were lustrous pearl studs, and she had a slightly weary but very self-possessed manner.

Her manner reminded Glenda of Edith, that of a woman who had never known hardship and who liked the amenities of life, such as breakfast served to her in bed and always on a tray covered with a speckless cloth. Who always wore a fresh nightdress each night, who used the best Ivory soap and liked her bathroom to always be immaculate though she wouldn't dream of even folding a towel herself.

'I'm told, my child,' Aunt Héloise held out a hand which was showing signs of arthritis, 'that you made a very striking bride. I should so much have liked to be there; the church in which you were married is quite old and picturesque, eh? But I shall see the photographs. I am told that a number were taken.'

'Yes,' Glenda smiled, and then because of that vague resemblance to Edith, especially towards the end when she was constantly in pain, she leaned forward and placed a kiss on the drawn cheek.

'My dear child——' Aunt Héloise looked rather taken aback, as if she had decided to be affable to the new member of the family but not affectionate. She turned her eyes away and her look said plainly that it was a little too bothersome for her these days to try

and make friends. Poor woman, thought Glenda. Her
life had been a cushioned one, but now she had pain to
deal with and it absorbed most of her energy.

Glenda was re-introduced to Rachel and Renée,
cousins of Mal's who had been at the wedding but who
had flown back to France on a tourist flight. They were
twins, but totally unalike in looks. Rachel, dark-haired
and smart, worked as a secretary for the Malraux
Company. But Renée, whose figure was more lush, had
branched away from the family business and worked
for a local *vigneron*. She had been rather critical of the
champagne served at the wedding, and Glenda recalled
that Mal had laughed and muttered that being sweet on
your employer didn't turn his wine into a superior brand.

'I so admired your wedding dress, Glenda.' Rachel
had a cool voice which matched her looks. 'Such a
simple style but so effective, especially with your hair.
It is naturally that shade of auburn?'

'Of course it's natural,' Mal said impatiently.
'Glenda's hair was exactly that shade when she met
Grandpère, just prior to his death.'

'*Je suis désolée.*' Rachel raised an eyebrow at Mal. 'It
seems I touch you on a nerve, but I suppose at the
beginning husbands are inclined to think their wives
beyond reproach, even when the marriage has been
arranged.' Rachel glanced back at Glenda. 'It isn't
quite the way of things in your country, eh? The
arranged alliance? You people believe in falling in love
before joining your lives together?'

'What makes you think,' Mal was looking steadily at
his cousin Rachel, 'that Glenda and myself are not in
love?'

'I never took you for the loving sort, Mal.' Rachel
gave a cool laugh. 'You have always been so wrapped

up in business—*ma chère* Glenda, who was that devastatingly handsome young man at your wedding, tall and fair, and wearing that superb uniform? I couldn't help noticing him! Once or twice I looked at him during the ceremony and he had his eyes—such very blue eyes—fixed on you. He's a close friend of yours?'

'His father was a close friend of my mother's,' Glenda replied carefully, feeling beside her the dangerous stillness of Mal's tall figure. 'He's the son of Sir Arthur Brake, who gave me away.'

'I see.' Rachel's dark gaze dwelt on Glenda's face. 'Isn't that a quaint English expression—do you feel as if you've been given away?'

'You ask too many questions,' Mal interposed. 'You should have entered the Inland Revenue service, my dear Rachel. Come, Glenda, and meet my sister.'

It was a relief to be drawn away from the inquisitive Rachel, who had obviously used her eyes at the wedding and drawn conclusions which she had used to needle Mal ... yes, Glenda told herself, that dark-eyed, outwardly chic young woman was inwardly churned up about Mal's marriage. It seemed more than possible that her affection for him was rather more than cousinly.

Glenda cast a quick look at him, seeing his forceful build and the dark power in his face ... the face which Rachel had known before the foundry fire had wrecked it.

Jeanne Talbot didn't resemble her brother, and then it struck Glenda that they seemed unalike because her hair wasn't black like his but almost silver. Her face was quite lovely, but there was such a lack of animation in her gaze that she gave the impression of being miles away in her thoughts.

Beside her on the tapestried couch sat a serious-faced young boy . . . when he raised his eyes from the book he was reading Glenda felt disturbed by the look in them. Never had she seen eyes so hauntingly sad in the face of a child . . . a child, she realised, whose mother kept him constantly by her side in case she lost him.

'This, Robert, is your new young aunt,' Mal informed him. 'I've an idea that you and she might become good friends.'

Don't, Mal, she wanted to implore . . . I'm leaving you, today!

'How do you do?' Robert stood up and gave her a formal bow.

'I'm glad to meet you, Robert.' Glenda was touched by the boy's serious good manners and by his air of being overlaid by cares beyond his years.

'Does the Château still seem to you the enchanted castle which you once called it?' Jeanne looked at Glenda in an apathetic way and there was no real interest in her voice, but her remark warned Glenda that here was someone else she was supposed to have met when she was a schoolgirl. Was Jeanne older or younger than Mal? It was difficult to assess her age because of the premature silvering of her hair, no doubt brought on by shock at the way her husband had died.

'The Château has an ageless beauty,' Glenda murmured.

'I think it might be a good idea after lunch for Robert to take you on a tour of the Château,' Mal remarked. 'You have to become reacquainted with your home.'

No, Glenda wanted to protest. This place will never be my home, because I shan't be staying!

'Perhaps Robert has something else he wishes to do

after lunch,' she said. 'Perhaps he wants to go out and play.'

Mal raised an eyebrow at her and his look seemed to say: 'You can see the kind of child his mother has turned him into! Playing and getting dirty like other boys is something he knows nothing about!'

'You can get your nose out of a book, my boy,' Mal said to him, 'and you can go exploring with Glenda. You can show her the stables and the weeping willow which is supposed to have grown up on the spot where they burned the wicked lord's little white witch. No doubt you saw the willow when you were a child, Glenda, but its legend would have meant less to you.'

'Very well.' She submitted to his dictate. 'But I—I would like to see you alone, Mal, later on today.'

'Would you?' His sardonic gaze held hers. 'We have all the time in the world, *ma chére*, but I'm flattered that you can't wait to be alone with me.'

CHAPTER FIVE

GLENDA gave a start as the dining-gong resounded in the hall and her arm was taken and threaded through Mal's. 'You must be ravenous for your lunch, so come along.'

There was no resisting his authority; there wasn't anything she could do right now but go with him into the dining-room where he seated her beside him at the large oval-shaped table. The room had long windows overlooking a court where a fountain sprayed arcs of water into the air and there was a sound of birds.

Glenda saw that the room was furnished in the French-Victorian style, which was possibly the era in which the Malraux family had first acquired the Château Noir.

Had Edith and her young daughter dined here after the marriage arrangement had been entered into with Duval Malraux, who had been determined to manipulate the future of the Malrauxs even as his own life was ebbing away? Glenda eyed Mal through the veil of her lashes and saw that he, too, was brooding among his thoughts.

She studied the menacing shadows of that Zurbaran-like face and told herself that all he needed was the monk's hood and the skull clasped in his hands in order to resemble St Francis in Meditation. On what was Mal meditating? Was he recalling the event which had shaped his future and brought him side by side with a wife who was still a stranger to him?

Glenda ate her cream of mushroom soup and listened

74

absently to Renée, who kept referring to a man named Jacques. 'Are we to hear about this wonderful *vigneron* all through lunch?' Rachel enquired suddenly.

'You're only jealous because there's no one interested in you.' A smile curled around Renée's lips as she eyed her sister across the table. 'We all know why you're disappointed, don't we, sister dear?'

'Close your silly mouth,' Rachel snapped. 'How any man in his right mind could be bothered with you, though I swear half of it is in your imagination.'

'Oh no, it isn't,' Renée rejoined. 'You're the one who's been kidding yourself——'

'Shut up, I tell you!'

'Now what is this?' Mal demanded. 'Can't you two ever agree on a single thing, and do you have to air your disagreement at my table? Glenda will conclude that she has married into a nest of hornets if the pair of you don't simmer down!'

'Why, is Glenda afraid of getting her lily-white skin stung?' Rachel drawled.

'Sting Glenda and you deal with me,' he told her.

'How masterful you sound, Mal, but do English girls like to be mastered? You sit there quietly, Glenda, but I wonder what is going through your mind?'

Glenda glanced up from her plate and found Rachel's dark gaze upon her. 'I wouldn't want to generalise,' she said. 'I expect there are English women who like a man to be dominant, so long as he recognises the fact that a woman is a person and not a possession.'

'Are you listening, Mal?' Rachel fondled her wine glass as she looked at him. 'I hope you're in agreement with what your wife says? You've always been a rather possessive man, haven't you, cousin? I believe you'd do anything to hold on to the foundry and the Château, even if it meant selling your soul to the devil.'

When he laughed and didn't argue with Rachel's statement, Glenda felt as if a cold finger brushed the nape of her neck. She could feel herself shrinking inwardly when Mal leaned towards her. 'Don't let your wine stand and grow still,' he said. 'Aren't you enjoying your lunch?'

'Of course——'

'Try some oysters.' They were large ones, in a relish sauce, laid out invitingly to encircle a large dish, segmented lemon at the centre. Mal placed several in front of Glenda and showed her how to prise them out of the shell, then in a little pool of the sauce how to swallow them. He invited young Robert to join in the game, while the boy's mother looked on in that anxious way of hers.

'Mal, don't let him choke——'

'My dear sister, will you let the boy enjoy himself for once!'

'I would blame you——'

'Of course you would, but it isn't likely to happen. Well, old chap, what do you think of oysters?'

'*C'est bon, mon oncle.*' Robert grinned, and with relish sauce all round his mouth he looked the carefree youngster he was meant to be.

'Robert, wipe your mouth,' his mother said sharply. 'Any more of those disgusting objects and you will be sick. I will not have you encouraging my child, Mal, to eat those vulgar things!'

'They were always much enjoyed by old Duval,' Mal said musingly. 'He ate some for his last supper and enjoyed them.'

'They probably helped him on his way,' Jeanne retorted.

'My dear, do stop being such a damp blanket!'

'How unfeeling you can be——' Tears filled Jeanne's eyes and she pressed a lace handkerchief to her quivering lips. 'You—you have a heart forged in that foundry you set such store by—I hope Glenda can endure you.'

'*Dieu*,' he exclaimed, 'women are the devil! Can we never have a meal in this house without some drama to accompany it? Glenda will begin to wonder if she can endure my family! Perhaps I should throw you out of the house and stop being the fool who keeps the lot of you!'

'And where should I go at my age?' his aunt asked plaintively. 'Take no notice of your sister, Mal. She tries to live with the dead, and as I sometimes say to myself she certainly isn't much company for the living.'

'Oh, for heaven's sake,' Renée groaned, 'can't we be lighthearted and pretend we all love each other?'

'There she goes with that word again,' Rachel drawled. 'You have love on the brain, but you'll learn, like everyone else, that it only exists in books of romance. That's why people enjoy reading them, because of the happy endings. Real life can't provide such a guarantee—look what happened to poor Jeanne!'

'Jeanne has to make an effort to forget what happened to her,' Mal said sternly. 'Now would every one mind giving their attention to the Quiche Lorraine? And who would like more wine?'

'I don't mind.' Renée held out her glass. 'But Jacques has produced a *vin blanc* you would truly enjoy, Mal. I will ask him on Monday to send you over a complimentary bottle.'

'That's very good of you, *chérie*.' Mal's smile was sardonic. 'I'm desolated that you find the wine from my cellar so inferior, especially in view of the fact that quite a lot of it was put down by old Duval, and he was a legendary connoisseur of wine.'

With a mocking glint in his eyes Mal raised his wine glass and studied the contents, then he put the glass to his nose and sniffed the bouquet. 'H'm, quite inviting, I think, but I'll bow to the superior knowledge you have gained from one year—one whole year of working with Monsieur Jacques. Whatever will you be like at the end of two years?'

Rachel burst out laughing and appreciatively raised her glass to Mal. 'Crossing foils with you is a risky business, *mon cher*. I think your tongue as well as your heart has been forged in the Malraux foundry.'

'No doubt it has.' He quirked an eyebrow at Renée. 'Don't run before you can walk, little one. I know you have enthusiasm for the wine business, but let me tell you that I've been studying the iron industry since I was a youth and I still don't consider that I know all I would like to know. Don't be too dogmatic. Permit others to be experts as well; it helps in business to be a diplomat even when we believe in our hearts that we know best.'

'All the same,' the blush which he had teased into Renée's cheeks was slow in dying, 'I'm glad I don't work for you.'

'*Touché*.' He inclined his dark head and turned to Glenda. 'Don't let it alarm you that this family likes to argue at the dining-table; you'll get used to it.'

'Will I?' she said, knowing very well that she had no intention of staying at the Château Noir as a member of his family.

'Of a certainty, *ma chère*.' He laid a firm right hand over her left one, a significant gesture in itself. 'Our bark is often worse than our bite.'

Glenda wished she could believe it. She anticipated

trouble when she told him she was leaving him. She owed him that courtesy and couldn't just walk out, leaving a note propped on the mantelpiece. In any case he wouldn't be easy to elude; as he had told her last night he was the local *seigneur*, and without the aid of a hired car to the airport she'd be stranded on his territory.

Knowing her to be Malraux d'Ath's wife, the people hereabouts wouldn't be in any hurry to help her get away from him. He was their landlord, so it was very unlikely that they'd invite his wrath ... and Glenda didn't doubt that, when angered, Mal could be very angry.

Dessert was a delicious plum tart with cream, and Glenda couldn't believe her ears when young Robert's mother said that he was to have a small piece of cheese and a couple of crackers instead of tart. Glenda met the boy's eyes and she spoke impulsively:

'Oh, do let Robert have some of this,' she pleaded. 'It is so nice, and it seems such a shame to deny him——'

'It would be a greater shame,' Jeanne said icily, 'if my son lost his teeth because of eating sweet things. I know what is best for Robert! When you have children of your own, Glenda, then you may indulge them as much as you like, and if they end up with dentures then that will be your concern. I want my child to grow up with good sound teeth—you will have noticed your husband's teeth. Mal will inform you that neither he nor I were permitted sweet things by our grandfather. It may seem harsh, but Robert knows I have his interests at heart, don't you, *chéri*?'

'Yes, Maman.' The boy dutifully ate his cheese and crackers and tried to look as if he wasn't yearning for plum tart, the deep red of the hot plums delectable with the thick ivory cream.

Glenda glanced at Mal, who met her eyes as he cut into his own piece of blue-veined cheese. 'Jeanne is right,' he said. 'Sometimes we have to know what is best for the young, whose eyes are not always the best guardians of their stomachs.'

'If you say so,' she murmured, rebellion in her eyes. 'It's my opinion that a little indulgence never hurt anyone. Edith often allowed me to have cream pastries and I don't wear dentures. So long as a child is taught to clean the teeth regularly, then where is the harm?'

'Each mother has to do things her way,' Mal said diplomatically, and a faint smile glimmered in his eyes as they rested on Glenda's face. 'I don't think I shall be too much the tyrant if you wish to feed our child on plum tart.'

His words sank ominously into her mind and she quickly lowered her gaze, hearing Renée give a laugh. 'You are a tease, Mal. You've only just started your honeymoon and already you're itching to be a parent. It's all right for men! They just stalk about looking proud while the poor wife gets all huge and cumbersome.'

'Do mind your talk,' Jeanne said sharply. 'We aren't a bunch of grape-pickers and we don't want a discussion of that sort at the table.'

'It's healthy,' Renée rejoined. 'At least those people enjoy their lives, which is more than can be said for you, Jeanne. You spend half your life in the family chapel lighting candles to the dead——'

'How dare you!'

'Well, it's the truth. No one wants anyone to die, but it is a fact of life that we can't call them back or share anything with them once they are gone. I know how much you loved Gilles, but he's gone, and you're still a young woman and you shouldn't go on acting as if your life is a—a sort of Greek tragedy!'

'Mal, do you hear how this girl speaks to me!' Jeanne's lace handkerchief was on display again, and so were the emotional tears. 'If any of you—any of you had suffered as I have——'

'Mal has!' It was Rachel who spoke, as if driven. 'His poor face bears witness to it—he didn't have to go back into that foundry after his foreman, but he went back in! He saved a life just as Gilles saved yours, but I can't imagine that Gilles meant you to be so miserable about it.'

'He must be turning over in his grave to hear me being spoken to in such a fashion!' Jeanne pushed back her chair and got to her feet. 'Come, Robert, I won't let you listen to such unkind things about your poor mother. You know, chéri, how I suffer, don't you?'

Robert was obeying his mother when Mal spoke. 'I want the boy to take Glenda on a tour of the Château,' he said firmly. 'I can't manage to escort her as I have paperwork awaiting me in the office, and apart from that I have to agree that you make yourself unhappy with your continual grieving. It isn't good for the boy, don't you realise that? Teeth! What are teeth compared to a sound mind?'

Jeanne gazed at her brother with shock and reproof in her eyes. 'I—I never expected you to turn against me, Mal, but I suppose now you have a wife you have no time for a mere sister. My poor broken heart makes you impatient, I can see it!'

'Nonsense, Jeanne. Be seated and have your coffee.

Be reasonable, *chérie*, and don't be so extreme about everything. Rachel is right when she says that we can't bury ourselves alive with the dead, much as we venerate them. Gilles was one of the best and he demonstrated that to the full, so feel blessed that you were loved by him and come to terms with his death. He would want you to do so, you know it.'

'Do I?' Jeanne stood there with despair on her face . . . once a beautiful face, Glenda realised, but grief had worn it away and there were delicate signs of ageing around the nostrils and the mouth. It struck Glenda that there had been great passion in Jeanne's love of her husband; a passion which probably ran in the veins of the Malrauxs, molten as the metal in which the fortunes of the family had been forged.

For Glenda it was a disturbing realisation that those strong passions were smouldering in Mal . . . the husband whom she didn't want. The husband whom she meant to discard.

'Jeanne, I insist that you cease to torment yourself because you didn't die with Gilles. It was decreed by fate—destiny—call it what you will.' Mal rose to his feet, dark and commanding in his black breeches and knee-boots, his thin silk shirt outlining the muscularity of his chest and shoulders.

Glenda could feel her heart thudding in her breast as he approached his sister and put his strong arms around her. 'Accept what was meant to be, *ma belle*. Accept or you will be destroyed by your self-inflicted pain, and then what will Robert do?'

Jeanne leaned her silvery head against the black silk of his shirt and her body shook with a visible tremor. He stroked her hair, his hand dark-skinned against the silver; the power in his body seemed to emphasise her fragility.

'I am not unfeeling, Jeanne, you have to believe me. This face of mine just seems to give that impression.'

'Oh, Mal——' His name seemed to be wrenched from her lips. 'Is this family cursed, do you think? Look at the way Maman and Papa died! I had nightmares about it when I was young. It was as though I was waiting—marking time for something just as horrible to happen again, and it did—it did! What next, Mal? Don't you wonder that I keep my son close to me? Wouldn't you do the same if you had a son?'

'I can't say.' His voice and his look were sombre. 'Of course you care for Robert, but you must allow him to enjoy his childhood or, my dear, he'll resent you when he becomes a man. You wouldn't want that, would you?'

'I—I want nothing to happen to him.' She turned her head and her great dark eyes fixed upon her son's face. 'He's all there is of Gilles and I have to make sure that whatever curse there is on this family——'

'There is no curse,' Mal said sternly. 'Tragedies happen in most families, as your common sense must tell you. Now have your coffee, then take a siesta while Robert keeps Glenda company. What harm is there in a pair of young people enjoying an afternoon together? You know, there is a saying, "the most wasted of days is that on which one has not laughed." '

'Ah, *mon ami*,' Jeanne sighed, 'the hours, the days are always so blue!'

'Then let some sunshine into your heart, *ma chère*, and it will grow lighter. You'll see.'

Jeanne looked unconvinced and with a sigh she sat down again. Robert took hold of her hand and gave

her a concerned look. 'It is all right, Maman, if I go
with Glenda?'

'Do you want to, *chéri*?'

'Well, I wouldn't mind too much.'

'Then you had best do as your uncle wants.' Jeanne
directed her gaze to Glenda. 'You will ensure that
Robert behaves himself.'

'I'm sure your son rarely misbehaves,' Glenda said
quietly, thinking to herself that it would do the boy
good to get up to some mischief and arrive home looking thoroughly grubby. She had to agree with Mal that
Robert's childhood was being spoiled by his mother's
nervous fears for his safety. He'd be as neurotic as
Jeanne if something wasn't done to prise him away
from her constant vigilance, and it would be a pity for he
was a nice child, with something in his smile . . . of course,
Mal would have looked something like him at that age,
except for a difference in the coloration of the eyes.

Mal had a darkly Latin face, which made his steel-
grey eyes seem extra penetrating. She didn't doubt that
as a young man he had been attractive enough for the
real Glenda Hartwell to have referred to him as a *preux
chevalier*, and it was the real Glenda who had appealed
to him. He remembered her as an eager young flirt,
candid about her longing to live at the Château, and
quite happy to have her life arranged for her. It was
tragic that someone so young should have died . . . was
it too ridiculous, the notion that those who came within
the orbit of the Malrauxs fell under a kind of cloud . . .
or curse, as Jeanne had called it?

According to legend a young woman, a so-called
witch, had been burned in the grounds of the Château.
Did some dark cloud from her pyre hang over the place
. . . oh, but that was absurd superstition, Glenda

chided herself. She was allowing her imagination to run away with her because Malraux d'Ath sat there with a fire-scarred face, and because Jeanne Talbot had narrowly escaped death in the arms of a husband who must have been dead when the rescuers opened up that crashed lift and lifted her out of his last embrace.

Yet, as Glenda's gaze drifted from Jeanne to Mal, she couldn't help thinking that it was remarkable the way tragedy had struck the occupants of the Château Noir. It was tempting to believe that the black castle was cursed for those who lived in it.

The family dispersed shortly after taking coffee and Glenda found herself being escorted around the Château by Mal's young nephew. 'Show me the willow tree first,' she had requested.

And now they stood beneath its weeping green boughs and it was strangely quiet, as if no birds came to sing in the tree. All at once a thin young hand crept into Glenda's and she glanced down to find Robert gazing up at her with solemn dark eyes.

'Are there witches?' he asked very quietly.

'Only in our imagination, Robert. We allow ourselves to believe in all sorts of fantasies, and in a way it's good for us. It shows us that our minds are active and that we aren't dull, unimaginative people.'

'You look like the witch in the picture in Uncle Mal's library,' the boy informed her.

'Thank you, young man!'

'She's very pretty, with red hair like yours.'

'You'll have to show me the picture, but right now what else shall we look at?'

They wandered about, across the velvety grass of a bowling-green to a small archery field beyond, and then along a path which led to the stables where some of the finest horses Glenda had seen were housed in well-kept stalls. A handsome sable head poked itself over one of the Dutch doors and Glenda fondled the animal, looking surprised when a voice called out to her to be careful

A bow-legged man in breeches came towards her. 'It does not do, *madame*, to touch Armide. That one has an uncertain temper and recently he had his teeth in one of the lads.'

'The horse seems quite tractable, *monsieur*. Perhaps the stable boy misused him.' She didn't withdraw her hand from Armide's head; she had been taught to ride soon after her adoption by Edith and had proved to be, like many another shy girl, a natural friend to any animal she came in contact with. She could feel the horse's response to her and was quite unafraid of him.

'Who rides him?' she asked.

'He belongs to the master, *madame*. It's unusual for Armide to take to anyone else.'

'He looks as if he can really go.' Glenda ran her hand down the black glossy neck and would have loved to take a gallop on such a horse. 'Is he an Arab?'

'*Mais oui, madame*.' The bow-legged man pushed his hands into the pockets of his breeches and gave Glenda a swift up-and-down look. 'The master might not let you risk your neck on Armide's back, and then again he might not wish to risk Armide's back with a woman in the saddle.'

She smiled. 'Don't you think I could manage the horse?'

'You might well manage the horse, *madame*; it's the master I'm thinking about.'

'Is Monsieur Malraux so to be feared?'

The man shrugged, and Glenda knew that he watched her and Robert until they were out of sight of the stables. The boy told her he was Restif Gerent who was in charge of the horses; that he came from Algiers where he had worked for Mal's parents.

'He is very loyal,' the boy said, in his old-fashioned way. 'Uncle Mal expects it.'

'He would,' she murmured, and tried to ignore the nervous tingle that travelled down her spine and seemed to make her legs feel shaky. She mustn't let thoughts of Mal unnerve her, not when she felt capable of handling an Arab stallion whose temper was uncertain.

'Where are we going now?' she asked Robert.

'To see the fishpond,' he replied. 'It is big and there are koi carp in it a foot long, and you should see them flash around. Do come!'

'You like fish, Robert?' They went down some stone steps and alongside low walls hung with tiny dancing fuchsias in scarlet skirts. From here the Château could be seen as if painted against the sky, and Glenda stood a moment gazing up at the place, taking in the fascinating corner towers corbelled out upon the silvery stone walls and capped by black spires.

Could a man be blamed for wanting to call such a place his very own? She supposed not, and felt she could have loved such a house, had she not been required to live in it with a man she didn't love.

The green shade of a lovely old fig tree made shadows on the pool where the golden carp darted through the reeds and under the lily-pads. Robert stretched himself out on the mossy bank and leaned over the water to watch the fish; he shot a mischievous smile up at Glenda, and gone for the time being was that air of being solemn young squire to his ailing mother, his youthful enthusiasms bottled up and never allowed to bubble over.

'Aren't they beauties?' He leaned eagerly close to the water. 'I'm going to stroke that one that's striped like a tiger—you watch me, Glenda!'

She watched, and refrained from telling him to be careful. It was a word his mother used too often to suppress his boyishness, but even as Glenda bit it back, there was a splash and a yell and Jeanne's son was in the pond with his beloved fish.

'Good grief!' Glenda threw herself down on the bank and reached out to grab hold of the boy. By the time she managed to pull him out of the pond he was wet as the fish and his nice white shirt was green as the water.

'That was a clever thing to do!' Glenda eyed him with dismay. 'Your mother will have a fit if she sees you looking like a half-drowned rat—come along, I'd better take you indoors and get you dried off.'

She marched him determinedly back towards the Château and wondered if there was a possibility of getting him dry and into clean clothing without his mother finding out. Jeanne would be bound to make more of the incident than was necessary and probably have hysterics. Her son wasn't allowed childish capers and was expected to behave like an obedient little robot. The very idea set Glenda's teeth on edge, even though she understood the root cause of Jeanne's behaviour. If she continued to restrict Robert he would eventually become a neurotic and sickly shadow of himself, and that would be a great pity.

Glenda glanced down at him and he gave her an

apprehensive smile. 'I—I didn't mean it to happen,' he said apologetically. 'I'm sorry——'

'It's natural for boys to get into mischief,' she reassured him. 'I expect your *maman* takes a nap in the afternoons, doesn't she?'

He nodded, wrinkling his nose against the water that dripped from his dark hair down his face.

'Do you think you can creep into your room and get a change of clothing without waking her?'

He sucked at his lips as he considered her question. 'I expect so—it wouldn't do to make her troubled, would it? Maman gets so upset about things and that's because of losing Papa when I was only three. Now she has only me to love.'

The remark was made in a touchingly serious way, and Glenda felt a sudden impulse of affection towards this little boy ... this child with the vague and troubling resemblance to Mal.

'Let's hurry,' she said. 'I don't want you to catch a chill.'

And like a pair of conspirators they hastened up the stairs and along the corridor which led to Jeanne's private suite. There in his extremely tidy bedroom Robert took clean clothes from his tallboy and then went with Glenda to the bathroom where he took a shower, had his hair dried, and was once again made spruce and neat.

Glenda dropped his soiled clothes into the laundry hamper and suggested that he take her to the library to show her the picture of the young witch with the red hair.

'Shall we ring for some tea and toast?' she said, as they made their way downstairs.

'I usually have tea with Maman in her room,' but

when the boy glanced up at Glenda there was a pleading in his eyes that she insist he have tea and toast with her.

'This is a bit of a holiday,' she smiled. 'I'm sure your mother won't mind if you spend all the afternoon with me. It will make a nice change for you, won't it?'

He nodded eagerly and escorted her across the hall to the tall doors of the library, which when opened revealed a large room whose walls were panelled in leather.

'It's very splendid, isn't it?' Robert murmured. 'You see the bear rug with the head attached?'

'Indeed I do.' Glenda glanced around her and saw handsome mahogany cabinets filled with books and fitted with mullioned glass. There were library tables with deep chairs beside them, a great Oriental rug underfoot, and a gigantic fireplace which in winter would burn large logs which would send showers of hot sparks up that black cavern of a chimney, its mantel made for tall men to lean against. Seated at one side of the fire-place was a stone salamander, with petrified flames around the creature. On shelves inside a buhl and tortoiseshell cabinet there was a collection of coins and gems and the silken hardness of small jade figures.

The windows rose from floor to ceiling and were hung with green and silver brocade, and beyond the windows there was the movement of grey clouds and the sense of a coming rainfall.

The room had an air of romantic melancholy, aided by a painting of a riderless horse bearing a pair of reversed boots, that most awesome symbol of a fallen leader.

'In the very olden days,' Robert informed Glenda, 'the horse used to be sacrificed at the graveside.'

'Do you read a lot, Robert?' she asked, her gaze wandering the leather walls in search of that other evocative painting ... the painting of the Black Castle witch.

'I like books,' the boy said, in his quaintly grave way, 'Maman likes me to read.'

Glenda was gratified to hear that the boy was allowed to do something he enjoyed doing. Poor mite, tied to the apron strings of a woman made morbid and possessive in her widowhood. It wasn't an unusual state for a woman to get into, but it usually meant that if a child was involved, then the boy or girl was trapped into a relationship which often sapped the joy out of being young and curious about life.

Even as these thoughts roved through Glenda's mind she found herself being drawn across the room to where a painting hung by itself in an alcove softly lit from above the antique frame. The face within that frame was creamy pale and medieval, with a long swathe of russet-red hair drawn back from the smooth forehead and cat-shaped eyes. The lips were full and faintly sulky above a chin indented at the centre. The girl wore a dress of green velvet, squared off her shoulders and showing a long slim neck encircled by a chain from which hung a pendant. Glenda leaned closer and saw that it was a tiny grotesque carved in amber-coloured stone.

'So this is the witch I'm supposed to resemble,' she said. 'I can't see a wart on the end of her nose, can you, Robert?'

'Like the one in *The Wizard of Oz*?' he laughed.

'That's the one.' Glenda turned away from the painting, for there was something disquieting in the realisation that the subject had been a real person who had perished in flames. Such horrifying things had taken place in the dim and distant past; young women had been dragged to a pile of kindling and set alight because they looked or behaved in a different way from their neighbours.

'It's going to rain.' Robert ran across to one of the deep windowseats and kneeled upon it. 'Look how dark the sky has gone!'

Glenda looked across and gave a sudden shiver. All that gloom would hasten the fall of dusk, and she had yet to tell Mal that she intended to leave the Château this very night.

'Let's ring for some tea!' She took hold of the thick silken bellpull and gave it a tug. 'It would be nice if we had a fire, wouldn't it? I think I'll light those kindling sticks under the logs and in no time at all we'll have a fire blazing merrily away—that is if I can find some matches.'

Beside one of the deep-buttoned leather chairs there was a table on which stood a carved box. Glenda opened it and found that it contained cigars, teak-coloured and strong-looking. These were probably Mal's, and there had to be matches around, for she had noticed that he lit his cigars with matches rather than a lighter.

She opened a drawer of the table and searched among the oddments which it contained. 'We're in luck!' The matches were in a folder bearing the airline name, tucked just under a slim, leather-bound book. Curious about Mal's taste in books, Glenda opened it and was rather surprised to find that it contained works by Robert Browning. No, she thought, Mal wasn't the sort to like poetry, but when she put the book to her nose and breathed the aroma of cigars she realised that it was Mal's.

Grown even more curious, she held the book to see if it fell open at a favourite verse ... it did, and her eyes wandered down the lines, pausing to take in something underlined.

> Where the apple reddens,
> Never pry—
> Lest we lose our Edens,
> Eve and I.

Glenda closed the book and shut it away in the drawer; she had pried and felt guilty about it. She felt sure it was a secret of Mal's that he, the man of iron, enjoyed the verses of Browning when he sat here in a fog of cigar smoke and let his thoughts stray along the London streets, to a certain house in Wimpole Street where Elizabeth Barrett had been swept from her invalid's couch by a determined and passionate poet. He had carried her down the stairs and out of the door and off to his beloved sunny Italy.

It was a romantic story, but Glenda would never have believed that it would appeal to Mal.

She knelt to kindle the logs, using three or four matches before the wood shavings smoked and flamed. How could she think of Mal as romantic when his reason for marrying her was such a mercenary one? He hadn't even bothered to come and court her. In his arrogance he had assumed that she would marry him, and here she was at the Château Noir to prove that Malraux d'Ath had a way of getting his own way.

She stared at the flames as they ran along the crisp bark of the logs. 'Burn, witch, burn!' they had chanted in the old days. No one stopped the lord of the manor from doing exactly what he wanted to do, and no one would stop Mal from doing what he liked with her.

She had to get away from him . . . him and his family. She didn't belong here, and she had to go before any of them found out that they had been tricked by her red hair into believing that she was Edith Hartwell's real daughter.

The library door opened and Glenda turned a startled head, her smooth red hair and pale profile outlined against the fire. It was one of the maids. 'You rang, *madame*?'

'Y-yes. We—Robert and I would like some tea and toast, please.'

'Very well, *madame*.' The maid glanced at the boy, who had sprawled himself out in the windowseat. 'Aren't you taking tea with your *maman*?' she asked, in a surprised tone of voice. 'Has she given you permission to have it down here?'

He looked at Glenda, who smiled reassuringly. 'It's perfectly all right,' she said to the maid. 'His mother knows that he's with me; in fact it was my husband who suggested that Robert and I spend the afternoon together.'

'I see, *madame*.' The woman hesitated. 'I don't mean to question your orders, but we're so used to the young master spending so much time with his *maman*.'

'I know how it is,' Glenda said quietly. 'Robert has been showing me over the Château and now we're both ready for a nice cup of tea and some crunchy toast. I don't suppose it matters if we have it here in the library?'

'I shouldn't think so, *madame*.' The maid glanced at the fire as if to say that it already looked as if the master's bride was making herself at home. She left the room, and Glenda sat there on the rug with her arms wrapped about her knees. The warmth from the fire felt nice, and she only wished that it was Simon who shared with her this fascinating old house rather than Malraux d'Ath. There would be no question of running away from Simon; his tall, fair, gallant image didn't arouse in her feelings of being threatened by dark forces in his nature.

Mal was so physically dark, and it seemed to add to the feeling of threat which she felt in his presence . . . which she had felt from the moment she had laid eyes upon him. He exuded a power and authority which didn't diminish with his absence; she had only to look around this leather-lined room in order to imagine him in it. Those shelves of books weren't there to furnish the walls, she felt sure he read them. Those prints and pictures had been chosen by him (all but the one of the red-haired witch) and it was obvious that he had a discerning eye. The ivory and jade pieces in the buhl cabinet would please his sense of touch and his Gallic shrewdness with regard to a good investment.

Glenda's arms tightened about her updrawn knees; the man who was her husband had a worldliness combined with the earthiness of the iron-master, but her own youth and inexperience cried out for the young man who had stood by, disciplined as only a soldier can be, and watched her become the property of the iron-master.

She bowed her slender neck and her red hair gleamed in the firelight . . . she yearned for Simon to come and rescue her, but knew that she must save herself from this loveless marriage.

CHAPTER SIX

THEY sat together on the rug and enjoyed slices of hot crunchy toast well spread with butter and plum jam. The tea had a slightly different flavour from the kind Glenda was used to, but it was hot and sweet and went down well with the plummy toast. She didn't dare to ask Robert if he was allowed to eat jam, but guessed from the way his mother had spoken at the lunch table that if she entered the library right now and found her son with jam round his mouth she'd march him upstairs and make him clean his teeth.

'Are you having fun?' she asked him.

He nodded, the huge dark pupils of his eyes catching the firelight. 'Is plum jam your favourite? Did you have it when you were a little girl and your *maman* was alive?'

Her mind sped back to the orphanage where the children rarely had jam on their bread; what a delightful surprise it had been when she went to live with Edith and tasted her first scones with dollops of cream and jam, eaten with the Darjeeling tea Edith had been so fond of. Often a poor sleeper, she would drink tea in the night; in the bedroom next door Glenda would hear the tinkle of the silver spoon in the bone china saucer and would picture the woman who had waved a kind of magic wand and wafted her away from the chilly building where there were no pink sheets on the bed and pillowcases with edging of lace. No soft sheepskin

96

rugs beside the bed and silky curtains that blew softly in the night and wafted into the bedroom the fragrance of wallflowers.

'Was your *maman* very nice?' Robert asked, watching her over the rim of his mug of tea.

'Oh yes,' Glenda said softly. 'She was very nice indeed.'

'Did she let you play with other children?'

The poignant query caught Glenda by the throat. It was selfishly cruel of Jeanne Talbot to deny her son the friendships that other children took for granted ... no love should be so possessive, for no human being was meant to be owned.

'Have you no friends of your own age, Robert?' she asked.

He shook his head. 'It's because I don't go to school,' he said practically. 'I have a tutor with whom I do lessons from Monday to Friday—he is a little strict and tells me that I am no good at maths. I try very hard, but I do them all wrong and he tells Maman I am a dunce.'

'I'm sure there are things you are good at, Robert.'

'I like to paint,' he said eagerly. 'Uncle Mal says I'm very good at painting horses.'

'You might well grow up to be an artist; would you like that.'

'I—I think I would, but I'm not so sure about Maman. She says she wants me to be a clever lawyer like my father was.'

'I expect that would please her, Robert, but we have to grow up to be ourselves, and if you're artistic, then it should be encouraged. Not every boy can draw a good horse. Do you go riding?'

'Maman won't let me——' He bit his lip, and then

said defensively: 'It's because she loves me and I'm her only child. Have you any sisters or brothers, Glenda?'

'No, I'm an only child like you, but my mother Edith liked me to go riding and I had a pony called Pieface.'

Robert burst into a laugh. 'What a funny name for a pony! Why did you call him that?'

'Because I was fond of him and he was rather sweet,' she smiled, her eyes softened by memories of rides through the woods at Barton-le-Cross, the snowy trees in winter and then in summertime those banks of azaleas and rhododendrons so gloriously tinted. How much there was to thank Edith for! A growing-up time she would never have known had Edith been a conventional woman, afraid to take a few risks in order to live with style ... admittedly at the expense of the Malraux family.

Dear Edith, no angel in the accepted sense of the word, but she had possessed the virtues of kindness and gaiety, and Glenda cherished her memory. It wasn't tarnished because of this unhappy marriage with Mal.

'It's fun giving our pets and friends a fun name,' she told Robert. 'What shall I call you?'

'I have to be called Robert,' he said, wrinkling his nose. 'Maman didn't like it when Uncle Mal started to call me Robbie.'

'Did you like being called Robbie?' Glenda asked.

The boy nodded and licked his jammy lips. 'But Maman asked Uncle Mal to stop calling me that and he did—he looked ever so angry and his black eyebrows looked as if they were joined together. When I grow up I want to shoe my own horses the way he does. He won't let anyone else do it, you know. He has his own smithy at the back of the stables and when he takes the horseshoes out of the furnace they're all glowing hot, and sometimes he lets me hold the horse still while he fits the shoes. It isn't at all painful for them, you know, not if it's done properly. Uncle Mal can do lots of things—I expect you're ever so pleased that he married you, aren't you, Glenda?'

'Over the moon,' she murmured, turning her gaze to the glowing heart of the fire. She had an image of Mal in his smithy, stripped to the waist in the smoking heat, his brown skin sheened with sweat as he hammered and refined the shoes for his horses. It was a primitive image which sent a strange little quiver through her and she hastily banished it from her mind.

She didn't want to be reminded of the dark, smouldering power which had been apparent even as Mal stood at the altar in his well-made suit. When he had taken her hand in his, her skin had looked blanched and her fingers so delicate that she had wanted to snatch them out of his clasp in case he broke them.

She pressed a hand to her mouth as if to stifle a little groan. She should have run from him before she ever spoke the words that were meant to be spoken only by a woman and a man who loved each other, body and spirit. There was sacrilege in it otherwise; guilt and trouble and pain.

Daylight was ebbing and the windows of the Château were filling with the red glow of the sunset. As the room filled with shadows and firelight, Glenda felt her courage ebbing away and she began to listen to the voice of caution that whispered in her ear.

Perhaps it would be wiser if she took the coward's way out and fled from her husband without asking his permission to leave him. She dared not stay! Mal had no love to give her, but he did care that the Malraux

d'Ath name be carried on, and that meant that he might
not leave her alone this coming night.

Sunset and fire seemed to bank up the fires of
Glenda's imagination and her mind began to smoulder
with images made all the more vivid by his behaviour
last night. She and Mal alone in that tower bedroom,
his big body looming over her, his arms reaching for
her, his iron-strong hands forcing her to comply. It
frightened her to remember how easily he had flung
her to the bed, no tenderness or mercy in his treatment.

Pride, not mercy, had sent him storming out of the
room when she had asked him to put out the light so
she didn't have to see his face.

It had all come back into her mind with such force
that when the door of the library was suddenly opened
she expected to see Mal framed in the opening. But it
was Jeanne who stood there, taking in the flicker of
firelight on the tea things, and her son sprawled on the
carpet and watching pictures in the fire.

Jeanne advanced into the room and her dark eyes
were venomous. Robert sat up sharply and Glenda felt
herself recoiling from the look on Jeanne's face. 'You
haven't been in this house two days and you're trying
to take my son away from me!' The words were choked
out and a flying hand sent the jar of jam crashing into
the hearth, plum jam spilling on the stonework among
shards of glass.

'Don't talk nonsense——' Glenda was appalled by
the naked anger and hurt in Jeanne's eyes. 'I'm doing
no such thing—as if I would!'

'I can see what you're up to, you little upstart! We
all know you've married my brother so you can have
the run of the Château! You got round our grandfather,

but you won't find it so easy twisting Mal around your little finger—and I'm not having you trying your tricks on Robert!'

She made to take hold of the boy, but obviously alarmed by her manner, he jumped to his feet and backed away from her.

'Do be reasonable.' Glenda rose to her feet, wanting to conciliate Jeanne for the boy's sake. 'All we've been doing is having tea together; what's so terrible about that? You were resting and——'

'Robert always has his tea with me, and he wouldn't be here with you if you hadn't enticed him. When I get him upstairs I'll teach him to stay away from you— I'll beat him for disobeying me like this!'

'You mustn't hurt him,' Glenda protested, and instinctively she went to the child and put an arm about him; he glanced up at her and his dark eyes were agonised. He was a mere boy and totally at a loss to understand a mother who at one moment was overwhelming him with her love, and the next moment was making demented threats of physical violence.

Glenda pressed him to her side, offering herself as shield and target. Her eyes held Jeanne's and she said as calmly as she could: 'You're not going to punish Robert for no reason at all—be reasonable, Jeanne, and let him have friends if he wants them. You can't possess him body and soul; none of us can do that unless we want to turn love into a burning resentment. Is that what you want?'

'Love?' Jeanne looked Glenda up and down scornfully. 'What would you know about love? Do you imagine that my brother thinks of you in that way? His marriage to you was arranged and it suited both of you for mercenary reasons. Everyone knew that Edith

Hartwell had no money of her own, so it's obvious she had precious little to leave when she died. Her generous allowance came from us. Grandpère bought and paid for you, and Mal will see to it that he collects on the deal, if you know what I mean. I'm not saying he will mind; with that hair of yours and those green eyes——'

Jeanne broke off in mid-speech and gazed narrowly at Glenda, whose face was illuminated by the last rays of the sun as they came streaming through the rain spattered windows for a few brilliant moments. Then that burst of radiance had gone and the room went shadowy and somehow menacing.

'I could have sworn that you had green eyes.' Jeanne took an abrupt step closer to Glenda. 'I remember that Grandpère remarked on them and gave you a little brooch shaped like a halfmoon and set with tiny emeralds. To match your eyes; those were his very words!'

Glenda's heart gave a nervous jolt; she had been scared all along that this would happen, that someone in this household would notice that her eyes were a different shade from those of the schoolgirl who had come here years ago in order to be looked over by Duval Malraux and pronounced suitable for his grandson when she grew up.

'How does it happen,' Jeanne asked curiously, 'that your eyes aren't green, the way I remember them?'

'I—really don't know.' Glenda strove to speak casually; if she showed any sign of nerves, then Jeanne would become even more curious. 'Blue eyes have a tendency to turn grey when their owners grow up, so I—I suppose mine have lost their greenness.'

'What about the brooch my grandfather gave you; do you still have that?'

'No, it was lost a long time ago—unfortunately.'
Glenda knew about the brooch, which Edith's daughter had lost on that last holiday they had together. It
had been pinned to the girl's blouse, but as she leaned
over the ship's rail one morning it had become
unpinned and had dropped into the sea. Edith always
said that it had somehow been a portent of tragedy,
that her child should lose the brooch and then fall
fatally ill herself.

'How careless of you to lose the brooch; it was very
pretty and I would have liked it, but Grandpère never
cared for me as he did for Mal. He was determined
that Mal should take over the iron foundry when he
grew up, so he got all the attention while I was ignored.
I ran off to Nice when I was eighteen and I took a job
in a hotel there, as a receptionist. I met my husband
there——'

Suddenly Jeanne threw her hands over her eyes and
a cry of pain broke from her. 'I can't stand it—I can't
stand it!' She turned and ran from the room, racked by
the grief that wouldn't stop torturing her. Glenda sat
down shakily in an armchair, her arm about Robert as
he buried his face against her shoulder.

'Poor Maman,' he whispered. 'Sh-should I go to
her——?'

'No, not just yet.' Glenda stroked the boy's hair, as
dark and lustrous as Jeanne's had once been until the
shock of her husband's death had streaked it with
white. Did Mal realise how close his sister was to a
complete breakdown, or was he too wrapped up in
running the family business to notice that Jeanne was
capable of some harmful action that might involve her
son?

Her arm tightened about the boy. Children were so

at the mercy of adults, who because of their own griev-
ances could inflict harm upon a hapless child without
fully realising what they were doing.

'Robert,' she said quietly, 'I think you and I must
go and talk to your uncle about your *maman*. You're a
sensible boy and I think you realise that she isn't being
very rational right now. You love her, of course, but
we can't allow her to do something that might hurt
you. Do you understand?'

He nodded and a sigh escaped him. 'Will my uncle
send Maman to a hospital?' he asked.

'I don't know, Robert. Perhaps it might come to
that,' Glenda had to admit.

'Then who will take care of me?' he asked plaintively. 'Will you?'

Glenda glanced over at the darkened windows;
beyond them night had fallen over the waterways
of the Loire Valley, over the Cher, the reed-
haunted Indre and the glistening green Vienne that
reflected the turrets and towers of Chinon. She knew
of these places only by reading about them; places
where Joan of Arc was part of the history and where
kings of France had built their castles, some as
sombre as a monastery, others as florid as a wedding
cake.

She had no personal knowledge of the Loire Valley,
and when night falls it has a way of mystifying even
well known places.

Robert was gazing up at her and because Glenda
had suffered from insecurity as a young child she
understood his feelings. 'I'm here, aren't I?' she said,
and her smile was hiding her own secret fears. It
seemed that tonight she must stay here; there were
other women in the house, but having met them she

somehow didn't think they understood the fears of a child as she did.

They seemed, each one of them, wrapped up in themselves, and it just wasn't in Glenda to leave Robert alone with them. His great-aunt was absorbed in her hypochondria, and neither of his cousins had struck her as having an abundance of sensitivity.

'Let's go and find your uncle,' she said, and together they went out into the hall, just in time to see Mal striding grimly out of the front door, which was flung wide to the rainswept night. His trench coat was flung on, the belt dragging, and he was carrying a large flashlight. Two of the menservants hurried after him, also in raincoats and carrying flashlights.

By the hall table where the telephone stood Rachel was trying to make a call and having difficulty getting through. Near the bottom of the stairs several of the maids were clustered together, whispering and looking alarmed in an excited kind of way.

Rachel finally gave up her attempt to telephone and she stood a moment frowning to herself.

'What's wrong?' Glenda demanded, feeling a clutch of foreboding.

Rachel glanced across at her, then looked at the boy in an hesitant kind of way. 'It's Jeanne.' Rachel ran the edge of her tongue around her lips as if they were dry. 'She's taken an overdose of something and run off into the woods—the woods are thick and they surround the Château—and it's raining like mad!'

There was an incredulous silence, then with a sob Robert wrenched his hand free of Glenda's and ran crying to the front door. 'Maman . . . Maman . . . I want you!'

'No, Robert!' Glenda sped after the boy, but he was

familiar with the great courtyard and he eluded her, running off into the garden in the wake of the men hunting for his mother.

Glenda came to a gasping halt, trying to get her bearings as the rain came down and plastered her hair to her neck and her dress to her body. Oh God, let nothing happen to the boy! She stood there feeling panicky and wet-cold. How desperate Jeanne must have felt to have done such a thing . . . in running off into the woods she seemed determined to end her life. Most suicide attempts were a cry for help and attempted within reach of someone to help before it was too late. This was different. The woods around the Château were thickly banked, and there was not a glimmer of moon or stars to help Mal and his men in their search.

Poor unhappy Jeanne, like a sick and disheartened animal she would fall down in the rain and perhaps die under the wet trees.

Shivering and soaked to the skin, Glenda found her way back to the Château. When she entered the hall Renée had joined her sister, and Mal's aunt was leaning back in a chair, holding her brow and looking as if the drama had been arranged to upset her. 'My nerves are in such a state that I don't know what to do about them,' she complained. 'My head aches and I have palpitations— how could Jeanne go and do such a selfish thing?'

'Selfish?' Rachel exclaimed. 'What are you talking about?'

'People who try and kill themselves are selfish,' Mal's aunt insisted. 'They just don't care about the worry and trouble they cause other people; they want everyone to be concerned about them and worried sick. Mind you, I've seen it coming. It's been pretty obvious for some time that Jeanne's unbalanced. I mean, we all have our crosses to bear—I've borne with bad health for years, but you don't find me getting hysterical and weeping about it and taking an overdose of sedatives.'

'She cared so enormously for Gilles,' Renée said sadly. 'He died so cruelly, and if it wasn't for Robert it might have been for the best had she gone with Gilles.'

'Do stop talking like a book,' Rachel snapped at her sister. 'Mal wanted me to phone Dr Corvelle, but I can't get through to him; sometimes when he's had a busy day Marie his housekeeper takes his phone off the hook; she shouldn't do it, but it's her way of ensuring the doctor some rest. I don't know what to do!'

'An unusual state of mind for you,' Renée rejoined.

'It's most inconsiderate of Jeanne to frighten us all like this.' Mal's aunt gave a sigh. 'If one is going to do that sort of thing, then at least one should do it in the privacy of one's bedroom so the entire household doesn't have to be disrupted.'

'Oh, stop it, the lot of you!' Glenda spoke with angry distraction. 'Don't any of you care that Jeanne's boy is out there in the darkness and the rain, running about like a scared little animal crying for his mother? What's going to be the effect on him if he finds her and she's— she's ——'

Glenda broke off helplessly, and it was obvious through the wet material of her dress that she was trembling.

'You're soaked to the skin!' Renée exclaimed. 'Have you been out in the rain as well?'

'I tried to stop Robert from running off, but he got away from me. I'm all right——'

'You'll catch your death if you don't change into

something dry,' Renée said with concern. 'Come up to my room and I'll find you a dressing-gown to put on—it could be hours, you know, before Mal finds Jeanne.'

'But what about Robert?' Glenda felt sick with worry, her hair in a draggled state about her wan face. 'What should I do about him? Mal put him in my charge and I feel responsible for him. Would one of you come with me to look for him?'

'I'll put on a raincoat and go and look for him,' Rachel said unexpectedly. 'Order some coffee, Renée, and have another go at trying to contact Dr Corvelle. I am wondering whether we should inform the police about Jeanne—what do you think?'

'I don't think Mal would want that,' Renée replied. 'If Jeanne's all right, and she could be, then it would only cause problems to bring the police in on the matter. She may have dropped most of the tablets down the loo in order to make it look as if she's taken the lot. An empty phial doesn't mean that she's swallowed them.'

'Until we know for certain, we have to assume the worst,' said Rachel. 'I'll go and see if I can track down that poor kid.'

She took a raincoat from a cupboard in the hall; also a trilby hat which she pulled firmly down over her brow. She went out into the rain, while Glenda gave in to Renée's urging and went upstairs with her to take off her damp dress and replace it with a fluffy dressing-gown. Renée handed her a towel so she could dry her hair.

'What a way for you to begin your life with Mal,' Renée murmured. 'All this has rather dampened your honeymoon, hasn't it?'

'Yes,' Glenda agreed. She wasn't going to confide

the truth to Renée, that a honeymoon with Mal was an occasion she was desperate to avoid . . . but certainly not at the expense of his sister's life.

Oh God, was it possible that Jeanne had believed that she was trying to lure Robert away from her? Suddenly a sense of guilt was added to Glenda's anxiety.

'Has Jeanne ever attempted to take her life before?' she asked.

'No, though everyone expected her to have a try at the time she lost Gilles. If the poor soul feels that she can't go on living without him, then this could be a genuine attempt.'

'What makes you think it isn't?' Glenda pulled a comb through her hair and gazed at Renée through the dressing-table mirror. Her slightly slanting eyes were pure amber as the lamplight reflected in the glass and caught her expression.

Renée gazed back at her, a fleeting puzzlement crossing her face. 'She dotes on Robert, as you may have noticed, and I can't see her leaving him an orphan. She practically never lets him out of her sight. It surprises me that she let him spend most of the afternoon with you.'

'She didn't like it.' Glenda went over to a window, drew back the drape and stared out at the dark and blustery night. 'She came into the library and caught the pair of us eating toast with jam on it. She accused me of trying to take him away from her, and then she threatened to give him a good hiding. Robert was so alarmed by her manner that he naturally turned to me—she ran out of the room crying, a-and now I feel as if I'm to blame for what she's gone and done.'

Glenda turned from the window and stood framed

against the ivory silk curtains, which threw her red hair into relief. There was no colour in her face except for the amber of her eyes.

'You mustn't take that attitude,' Renée said. 'Jeanne doesn't like anyone to make overtures to Robert. She's even had arguments with Mal when he's tried to persuade her to be less of a mother hen forever clucking over her infant and stifling his natural urges. Heaven knows what he'll be like when he grows up, poor little scrap. It wouldn't suit Gilles, what Jeanne is doing to that child.'

'She lives in fear that something will happen to him——' Glenda broke off worriedly and gnawed her underlip. 'I—I hope they find her soon and she's all right. What she needs is treatment to try and cure her sense of anxiety—Mal must have realised that her behaviour was unnatural.'

'Mal knows what she's been through; I don't suppose he wanted to add to her suffering,' Renée said, giving Glenda a slightly resentful look. 'You might have married him, but you don't really know him, do you?'

'That isn't exactly my fault,' Glenda retaliated, a flush of colour warming her cheeks. 'He never once came to Barton-le-Cross but just took it for granted that I'd marry him when the time came. I'd say that was rather arrogant of him, wouldn't you?'

Renée shrugged. 'You didn't have to go through with it, but as people were saying at the wedding, it was an advantageous marriage for you, especially as your mother had died and her income reverted to the Malraux estate.'

'So all of you think I'm on the make!' Glenda exclaimed. 'I suppose it wouldn't occur to any of you

that I—I promised my mother I'd marry Mal, just as
he promised his grandfather. In his case, it was advantageous for him to marry me; by doing so he inherited
the Château. That was the icing on the wedding cake
for him!'

'I should think Mal himself would be icing on the
cake for most girls,' said Renée frowning. 'He's been
good to Rachel and me, so I'm not going to run him
down. It's true he can be arrogant at times, but what
woman wants a soft-centred man? Or are you a bit in
love with that fair-haired soldier who was watching
you so intently as you married Mal? Go on, you can
tell me. I'm not like Rachel; I'm a little more romantic.'

'Simon's very nice,' Glenda said noncommittally.
'Oh, I do wish we could hear some good news about
Jeanne! Shall we go downstairs and have some coffee?'

Glenda made for the door before Renée replied,
hurrying down the stairs away from the other girl's
curiosity about her. The big oaken door of the Château
was still wide open and the wind was blowing rain in
over the step. Otherwise the hall was empty, except for
the armoured knights bowed over their swords ...
rather like mourners, Glenda thought, shivering.

Holding the dressing-gown closely around her, she
went and stood in the doorway, feeling the whip of the
wind as she gazed out; feeling a bleak sensation at her
heart.

'Please God,' she prayed, 'let them be safe. Don't let
there be any more sadness.'

'Don't stand there getting cold,' Renée called out.
'Come into the *salon* and have your coffee.'

'In a minute,' Glenda said over her shoulder. 'I think
I saw a flash of light among the trees—the men might

be coming back—they might have found Jeanne.'

Renée came to her side and they watched anxiously as the beam of light broke through the shrubbery and stretched across the courtyard. When the group came within the orbit of the porchway light, Mal could be seen carrying an ominously still figure.

Renée clutched Glenda's arm painfully. 'Oh no!' she breathed.

Mal came into full view and his scars had a bitten-to-the-bone look beneath his black hair plastered wetly to his skull. Rachel walked just behind him, holding Robert firmly by the hand. His small face was streaked with tears, Glenda noticed.

'Robert must be taken care of,' Mal said as he carried his burden into the hall.

'Jeanne——?' The name died away on Glenda's lips.

He looked grim. '*Le bon Dieu* knows! Has the doctor been summoned?'

'We couldn't get through to him—I'll go and try again!' Renée ran over to the telephone and almost knocked it off the table in her agitation. Rachel let go of Robert's hand and shook her hair loose from the trilby hat. Glenda silently held out her arms and Robert ran into them, pressing his trembling young body close to her.

'It's all right, darling.' She cradled him in her arms. 'I'm going to take you upstairs and you're going to have a nice rub down, then a nice hot drink. The doctor will come soon, so don't worry.'

'Poor little Maman,' his brimming eyes looked up at Glenda. 'Uncle Mal couldn't make her breathe, he tried and tried——'

'You come with me, there's a good boy.' She urged him across the hall and up the stairs feeling certain there was nothing more to be done for Jeanne. Her lolling head and the ashen look of her skin held out little hope that she was still alive, especially as Mal had tried mouth-to-mouth resuscitation and there had been no response.

At the top of the stairs Robert hung back and gazed desperately down into the hall, watching as his uncle carried his mother into the library. Glenda's heart ached for the boy. He would never forget this night; it would imprint itself on his mind and he would always remember the way his mother had run off into the woods to die, and he would always wonder if he had been to blame.

His gaze lifted beseechingly to Glenda. 'I didn't have tea with Maman today,' he said sadly. 'Do you think that's why she—did it?'

'No, sweetie.' Glenda wrapped an arm about his shoulder and drew him away from the staircase. 'You mustn't think you had anything to do with the way your *maman* felt. She's been a sad and lonely woman ever since she lost your father, and you have to understand that she has never stopped wanting to be with him. She loved him very much, and she didn't mean the things she said to you. When we're unhappy we often say things we regret, so you mustn't go blaming yourself. Will you promise me that you won't?'

He nodded, his young face pinched and white. They entered his room and he quietly submitted to being dried off and put to bed. He removed his wristwatch and carefully laid it on the bedside table, and Glenda saw him lick away some teardrops.

'Comfy, Robbie?' she asked, settling the supper tray which one of the maids had brought to his room.

'Yes, thank you, Glenda,' he said, in his polite way.

'Going to eat your boiled egg and bread and butter?' she coaxed. 'I'll cut the bread into fingers, shall I? Then you can dip them in your egg.'

'Maman says only babies have that done,' he replied.

'Well, we all like to be babied now and then,' she proceeded to slice his bread and butter into fingers. 'I know I do, especially when I'm rather unhappy.'

'Were you very unhappy when your *maman* died?' He tapped the top of his egg with his spoon and carefully picked away the pieces of shell. 'Did you cry a lot?'

'I was very sad, but my poor mother was very ill and in lots of pain, so her death came as a release from all that. I saw how peaceful she looked, all the pain smoothed away from her face so she looked beautiful again. Death isn't terrible, Robbie. It's a kind of going home, and we all go there to rest when the time comes.'

'There must be lots and lots of people there,' he said, dipping a bread finger into the yolk of his egg. 'Doesn't heaven get terribly overcrowded?'

'Our spirit goes there, Robbie. This body that we leave behind doesn't matter any more; it's just the casing around that very special place inside us. Some people call it the soul. It's that, Robbie, that flies off into infinity and joins up with the spirit in the persons we have loved.'

'Really and truly?' he asked, fixing her with his great dark eyes.

'I wouldn't tell you anything that I didn't believe in myself,' she assured him. 'Is it a nice egg—it looks very nice?'

He nodded, but as he ate his supper Glenda noticed

that he kept glancing at the door adjoining into his mother's bedroom. Oh lord, she should have realised that the child couldn't spend tonight in the vicinity of Jeanne's room, even though she had planned to stay with him, wrapping herself in a rug in the wicker armchair beside his bed.

'Would you like to come and sleep in the Tour Etoile tonight?' she asked him casually. 'I have this comfy couch in my bedroom and I feel sure you'd enjoy sleeping in a tower, wouldn't you?'

'Won't Uncle Mal mind?' Robert watched her over the rim of his Ovaltine mug, a look in his eyes which told her it was what he longed for.

'I'm positive he won't. Now finish up your drink and I'll go and fetch your toothbrush and things from the bathroom, and you'll need clothes for the morning.'

He nodded and slid out of bed, replaced his wristwatch, then his dressing-gown and slippers. A few minutes later they were on their way downstairs, where Rachel was sitting in one of the carved chairs smoking a cigarette. When she caught Glenda's look of enquiry, she gave a moody shrug.

'I'm taking Robbie over to the tower for the night,' Glenda explained.

'Good idea.' Smoke slid from Rachel's lips. 'The doctor's here and he's ordered an ambulance. Jeanne's gone into severe shock and has to go on one of those life-support machines—thank God they're equipped for it at the local clinic. Mal supplied the money, ironically enough.'

'Is Maman going to—die?' Robert drew close to Glenda and she could feel his young body trembling.

'She's very sick, Robbie, but everything possible will

be done to help her get well,' Glenda assured him, going tense all through her body as Mal suddenly emerged from the library, thrusting the black hair back from his brow as he crossed the hall to stand and look down at her and the boy.

'I'm sorry, Mal,' she said quietly.

'She had no right to go to such extremes.' He reached for his nephew and lifted Robert into his arms, brushing his lips across the boy's thin cheek. Glenda watched them and saw again that elusive resemblance, then as Mal turned his face to look at her she saw only his scars, etched with cruel clarity because his face was so tiredly drawn and anxious.

'You're taking care of Robert?'

'Yes, Mal. I thought he should sleep in my room tonight.'

'I agree.' He cradled the boy against him, the tired young head drooping against the bone and muscle of that shoulder which had pillowed Jeanne's ashen face.

'I shall be going with Jeanne to the clinic; the next few hours will be crucial—*Dieu*, why should she go and do such a thing? I've done my best to make her feel at home here.'

'Perhaps she thought things would change now you're married.'

He swung round to look at Rachel, who had made the remark. 'There was never any question of things changing. Why should they?'

'Wives have been known, Mal, to want their households and their husbands to themselves. I don't think I'd want to share my husband with a clutch of relatives, especially when they have a habit of burdening you with their problems. A new young wife could find that—distracting, wouldn't you agree?'

'For heaven's sake, Rachel, you're talking as if Glenda and myself are starry-eyed romantics who long to be alone with each other!'

'You might have sown your first flush of ardent oats, Mal,' Rachel paused upon his name, almost suggestively, 'but Glenda is still young and romantic, isn't she? Why should she be obliged to share the Château with your ailing aunt, your unhappy sister, and a pair of rather impecunious cousins?'

'Don't let's confuse the issue,' he said cynically. 'As everyone is well aware, our marriage is one of mutual gain and convenience. Glenda and I entertain no illusions about each other—is that not so, *ma chère?*'

He flicked his gaze back to Glenda so quickly that he caught the stunned look in her eyes; she felt hit on a nerve by his brutal candour, but of course she had earned it. He had none of that polite veneer which allowed a woman's remarks to bounce off his ego without leaving a scratch. He was totally unlike the men she had met in Edith's company, who regarded women as amusing and capricious and best dealt with in a tolerant manner which made allowance for the fact that they were emotional; that they had fears which men never felt.

Glenda felt as if Mal had slapped her in front of Rachel. He either didn't know or didn't care that his cousin looked gratified; it was what she had been angling for, an admission from him that his marriage meant nothing to him.

'No illusions whatsoever,' Glenda agreed in her coolest tone of voice. 'Robbie is falling asleep on your shoulder, Mal. Are you going to carry him over to the tower, or shall I take him?'

'I'll take him—come along.'

The rain had stopped, but there was still a wind that whispered along the stone walk and up the winding stairs to the tower apartment, which as they stepped into it had again that private, shut-away-from-the-world atmosphere.

The lounge light was relaxing, stealing out from beneath gold-shaded lamps that threw a warm glow over the furniture. The dark and dismal night and its memories were shut out by warm-toned curtains, and there was the realistic glow and warmth of the electric fire.

Glenda paused in front of it, but Mal made for the bedroom stairs. She followed and he carried Robert to the big fourposter and slid him between the turned-back covers. It made little difference, she thought. It wasn't a night for sleeping and she'd make do on the couch.

'I think his dressing-gown ought to come off,' she suggested.

Mal nodded and carefully removed it. The boy was more than half asleep, snuggling his cheek into the pillow and ready to drift off into dreamland where, probably, he would stay until morning.

'The poor little chap looks worn out.' Mal stood at the bedside gazing down at his nephew. 'You shouldn't have let him get out of the house!'

'I tried to stop him, but he got away from me. I'm sorry, Mal.'

'Anyway, after a good night's sleep that business in the woods will seem less horrific for him, and it's better for him to sleep over here.' Mal leaned over the boy. '*Dieu te bénisse*, Robert,' he murmured.

The boy's eyelashes fluttered. 'Will Maman get well?'

'If *le bon Dieu* wills it, young one. Say a little prayer for her.'

The boy sleepily did so, then his heavy eyelids closed. 'G'night, Glenda,' drifted from his lips.

'Sleep tight,' she whispered, and as she kissed his cheek a tear crept from beneath his eyelid. There was an aching in her throat when she left the bedroom with Mal and they went down to the lounge.

Mal studied Glenda as she sat down in a chair, a ray of lamplight showing the tiredness and distress in her face. 'I think we both need a cognac,' he said. 'I think I've time—we shall hear the ambulance when it arrives.'

'Your poor sister,' she murmured, as he poured out the cognac and placed one of the brandy bowls in her hand.

'I should have seen it coming, but it isn't the sort of thing one likes to expect.' He tossed cognac down his throat. 'We aren't having a very propitious start to our marriage, are we, one way and another?'

'Hardly.' She held her own bowl between her hands and the aroma of the cognac drifted upwards, making her feel faintly nauseated. She didn't really want hers, but she had seen that Mal needed it.

'You didn't much like what I said to Rachel, did you?' His eyes were a flick of steel over her face.

'I could hardly object, Mal. We've married each other for all the worst sort of reasons, so the sooner I go——'

'That's the ambulance!' Mal swallowed the remainder of his cognac. 'You stay here and make sure that boy stays where he is. I'm going to the clinic and I shall stay with Jeanne for as long as it takes.'

'Mal,' Glenda jumped to her feet, 'I do hope—oh, I

pray that she'll be all right!'

He nodded curtly, then was gone, slamming the door behind him. With a sigh Glenda resumed her seat; there was nothing she could do but remain here and make sure that Jeanne's boy was all right. She set aside the brandy bowl and leaned back in her chair; she sighed sharply. The sound of the approaching ambulance had muffled her words so she didn't think Mal had heard her remark that she was going, as soon as possible.

In any case it would be callous of her to leave the Château Noir right away. There was Robert to consider. Glenda realised that he had taken a liking to her; that he trusted her, and that was more essential right now than her own adult concerns.

Adult? Perhaps foolhardy was a better word for what she had brought upon herself. But like Robert she had needed to trust someone when she was a child; to feel secure in the care of someone who cared. It didn't matter that Edith Hartwell's motive had been basically selfish; having taken on the responsibility of a foundling she had done her very best for the gawky little Welsh girl whom she had renamed Glenda Hartwell.

Glenda returned quietly to her bedroom to make sure the boy was still asleep and hadn't been awoken by the ambulance which had come to take his mother to the clinic.

No; worn out by the unhappy events of the evening, the child lay deeply asleep. Glenda didn't turn out the lamp; if he had a bad dream and awoke in the dark in a strange room he would be frightened, and in the next few days he was going to have worries and fears that a little boy shouldn't have to face.

She took a chair and sat by the window, the curtain

pulled aside so she could look out and see the lights from the main bulk of the Château. What a rambling place it was! The eyrie of Malraux d'Ath, set high above the haunting beauty of the Loire Valley, the castle he had set his heart on even though it had meant marrying a girl he didn't love.

Her thoughts winged their way to England and to the tall, soldierly figure of Simon Brake. What was Simon doing right now? Was he at Chelsea Barracks, or had he taken some leave and was at home in Yorkshire, galloping across the moors and maybe thinking of her?

Was he thinking of her? Was he wondering what sort of a life she was having with Malraux d'Ath? She was married to Mal, and if Simon truly cared for her, then it must cause him pain to have to imagine her in the arms of her husband.

Glenda's fingers groped upwards, finding the soft base of her throat where the anxious beat of her heart could be felt against her fingertips. Her need for Simon had never been more acute; she longed for his protective arms around her and his assurance that they would find a way to be together. Vague and disturbing was the thought that Simon might not be as ruthlessly determined as Mal at getting what he wanted.

Under her fingers she felt her heart leap. The more she saw of Mal, the more she noticed the dominance in him, and with all her heart she wanted Simon to stand up to him, to look him straight in the eye and say that she couldn't stay with a man who had married her so he could satisfy the demands of his grandfather's will and obtain absolute control over the Malraux Company.

Marriage to her made him master of the Château

and the land it stood upon. Now he was in absolute charge of the foundry and the metal works; made so by that wilful clause in the will of Duval Malraux. The other grandson, Matthieu, had a directorship and a solid income from the Company, but Mal had the authority.

It was his authority which Glenda feared, combined with the power of his personality and the physical darkness so in contrast to Simon's fairness.

He was like the night out there, where menace might reach out from among the trees and follow without sound the woman who walked there unguarded. In deepest shadow a hand would touch her, and screaming without sound, she would know there was no escape.

Dark ... dark like fate which always waited a few steps ahead of everyone's hopes and expectations. A dream could be glimpsed, the future planned, but there was no guarantee that the dream would become a reality.

Oh, Simon ... his name was a quiet groan on Glenda's lips. Why had he stood there in the church, silent and pale as marble, and let what had only been a shadow become a dark and solid presence between them? Had she hoped—yes, she *had* hoped that her golden Guardsman would leap forward to push aside the dark intruder and claim her. She had waited and waited, and then it was too late, and in a daze she had found herself walking to the vestry with Mal, her arm drawn through his ... his instead of Simon's.

She stared out into the darkness where up among the battlements a night bird settled, squawking as its claws closed upon the stonework. Behind her in the great bed Robert muttered something in his sleep. She rose and went to the bedside and for a long time she stood and studied that clear-cut profile against the pillow, the hair above it dark as a night bird's wing.

A child of Robert's age was so dependent upon adult behaviour, and there were shadings of fear even in the loving in case it be withdrawn, or become cruelty in place of kindness. How a child adored kindness; the hugging which was truly protective and loving. A child would do anything if given that in childhood.

At the age of nine Glenda had been led from the bleak boundaries of an institution where a hug and a kiss were unknown treats, and where a child's narrow iron-framed bed stood alongside dozens of other beds exactly like it, in a dormitory where the lights went out at the same time each night and where talking in bed was forbidden after lights out. Little chatterers who broke the rule had to write out three hundred times: *Speech is silver, silence gold. I must sleep when I am told.*

A warm and generous hand had led Glenda out of the gates and into a car so luxurious it had left her tongue-tied.

That slim, scented hand had led her through time to the Château Noir . . . this castle which was supposed to be cursed. Out on the turrets the night bird squawked again and Glenda glanced nervously over her shoulder, giving a start as her own reflection stared back at her from a cheval glass fixed to a frame.

She seemed framed like that painting down in the library . . . dark red hair against the creamy paleness of her skin, her eyes wide with apprehension, her lips startled.

It had been a strange day fraught with trouble, and she was letting her imagination run away with her. But at the end of such a day it was all too easy to imagine that a girl who died amid flames and black smoke had cried a curse upon all those who came to live in this château of silver-grey walls and black-capped turrets.

So beautiful by daylight . . . so menacing when night crept out of the woods and came close to the windows.

CHAPTER SEVEN

FOR more than a week Mal's sister lay in a coma, and he stayed at the clinic in the anxious hope that she would regain her will to live. Each day Rachel took him a freshly laundered shirt and other clothing he required and brought back messages regarding Jeanne's condition.

When relayed to Robert these messages were more hopeful than truthful; and all through those waiting days Glenda took care of the boy and did her utmost to keep him from brooding. They went for walks; she read stories to him and they played word games and did jigsaw puzzles. His tutor was told not to come and give him lessons until his mother was out of danger; how could the child be expected to concentrate on lessons, Glenda said, when he was sick with worry?

The boy wanted to go and see his mother; he begged Glenda to take him, but Mal had given orders that Robert wasn't to see his mother in her present state; it would be frightening for him to see Jeanne attached to a machine that was assisting her to breathe and function.

One morning, however, Robert concealed himself in the back of Rachel's sports car. If he hadn't sneezed his presence might have gone unnoticed and there was a good chance he might have got into the clinic. Rachel had to drag him out of the car; his yells brought Glenda running out of the Château, and it took the rest of the morning to calm him down.

'W-why can't I go?' he sobbed. 'I w-want to see Maman—and I hate you because y-you won't let me go to her!'

'You'll see her when she's feeling better,' Glenda assured him. 'Right now she's doing a lot of sleeping; you don't want to disturb her, do you? You know, people need lots of sleep when they're sick.'

'What if she wakes up and asks for me and I'm not there?' He wouldn't be consoled, and the depth of his misery struck a cold little chord inside Glenda.

She couldn't help but remember her own insistence on remaining at the hospital on what turned out to be Edith's last night on earth. No one, not even Simon, could persuade her to leave Edith's bedside; it was as if her heart was telling her that soon they must say goodbye.

Around noon, on the day Robert was so restless and upset, Glenda decided that it was more cruel than kind to keep the boy away from Jeanne, despite her grave condition. She impulsively rang through to the garage and told the chauffeur to be prepared to take Robert and herself to the clinic. She then told the boy where they were going and warned him that his mother was undergoing intensive treatment and would look very ill.

'Your uncle is going to be very angry with me,' she added, and she tried not to look as apprehensive as she felt. 'You must promise me to be a sensible boy; you're just going to have a peep at your *maman*, remember, and then we'll drive home again. You won't let me down, will you?'

'Why will Uncle Mal be angry with you?' he wanted to know.

She straightened his tie and smoothed his hair and thought how nice he looked in his smart dark suit and pale-blue shirt. 'Because he doesn't like people to disobey his orders.'

'But you're not people, Glenda.' Robert scanned her face in a puzzled way. 'You're Uncle Mal's wife, so I don't think he'll be angry with you.'

'I'm afraid he will be,' she said wryly.

As they went downstairs Robert gave her a couple of mystified side-glances. She could guess what was puzzling him. His father and mother had adored each other and had probably demonstrated this in front of him. He thought that all men treated their wives adoringly, and that all wives clung to their husbands and hung on to their every word. Some people were possessed by love, but Glenda wasn't certain that it was wise to so absorb yourself in another human being that life had no meaning without that person.

She knew she loved Simon, but not with a constant, gnawing hunger for him. She admired his appearance, and it was exciting to watch him out on the polo field. They shared the joy of riding across the moorland and they laughed easily together. She believed firmly that love had to be a companionable experience. Great tides of emotion could drag you down where you were at the mercy of your own despair . . . as Jeanne was.

Glenda and the boy settled themselves in the Renault and off they went, driving through the lovely countryside of the Loire.

The deep and gliding Loire, the longest of French rivers, wending its way through some of the most charming scenery in the world. Magnolias and medlars mingled together in the soft air; fruit trees and chestnuts grew in abundance out of the rich soil.

Such a summer-gold day, Glenda thought sadly, to be taking a child to see a mother who hung so precariously between life and death. Robert sat there quietly, gazing out of the car window as they drove over the cobbles of a village street, watched by women who sat at their bobbins making lace ... lace for wedding veils and lingerie, emerging in all its intricate charm from under the skilful fingers of lace-makers who resembled figures in an old master painting.

Glenda gazed back at them fascinated, and felt a world away from Barton-le-Cross, bucolic in a very English way, where the Tudor manor house dominated the village instead of the turreted walls and towers of her husband's château.

Her husband ... the very word made her heart feel trapped by quivering cords, tightening, making her feel breathless as the car approached the gates of the clinic.

A hand stole into hers and she glanced down at Robert's pale face and apprehensive eyes. It was no use, she thought, questioning the wisdom of this visit now they had arrived and the chauffeur was opening the door beside her. 'We shan't be long,' she said, and her voice was low and husky. He touched the peak of his cap and watched them as they entered the building that ambled around a courtyard where some of the patients sat on seats, chatting together or reading books.

Just inside the central doorway of the clinic there was a glass-partitioned office, and Glenda tapped on the door and was invited to enter. She explained to the woman behind the desk the reason for their visit and they were invited to sit down while a telephone call was put through to the intensive care unit. 'I must enquire, you understand,' the woman explained, giving

Jeanne's boy a sympathetic look.

Glenda sat there tensely while the woman made her enquiries. Her heart was filled with twin dreads ... that Mal would furiously enter the office, or they'd be told that Jeanne's condition had worsened.

The minutes ticked by, and Glenda almost jumped out of her skin when the office door opened ... to admit an orderly and not the tall figure of Mal demanding to know why she had disobeyed him.

'Madame d'Ath?'

'Y-yes.'

'Please to come with me.'

'May I bring Madame Talbot's son?'

'It is in order, *madame*.'

'*Merci*.' She took Robert by the hand and they followed the white-coated orderly along a corridor and up a flight of stairs to another long and winding corridor. Glenda could feel the nervous beat of her heart and Robert's small, clinging fingers. Was it a good sign or a bad one that the boy was being allowed to see Jeanne? Was Mal aware that they were here and would they find him with his sister?

The orderly came to a halt in front of a pair of swing doors; he held one of them open so Glenda and Robert could precede him into the unit, where each bed was concealed by a partition of impenetrable material on curtain-rings so it could be swept back and forth very quickly. Bleeping sounds were coming from an array of electrical equipment, and behind one of the curtains someone was groaning.

Robert's fingers gripped Glenda's as they were led to one of the cubicles ... she was thinking wildly to herself that she had been wrong to bring him to such a place, where patients lay more dead than alive, the frail beating of their hearts monitored by machines.

The orderly drew aside the curtain which concealed Jeanne's sickbed . . . Glenda's gaze was drawn at once to the daunting figure standing by the bed. In those seconds all she was aware of was Mal, his features sculpted hard and almost unrelenting; feeling as if she had pieces of ice in the very pit of her stomach, she met his eyes and caught their glimmer of irony beneath the black gabling of his brows.

'Please understand,' she said huskily. 'Robbie was making himself ill wanting to see his mother——'

'So you decided to bring him despite my instructions?'

'Yes.' She pulled her gaze from Mal's face and glanced down at the boy, who was staring at the still and pallid figure of his mother. One of her nostrils had a tube inserted, and an inverted bottle fixed to a stand was feeding a colourless liquid into a vein of her arm.

'As you can see,' said Mal, 'Jeanne was taken off the life-support machine last night. I didn't inform any of you. I felt it better to wait in case false hopes were raised . . . I spoke with her doctor an hour ago and he feels confident she will now pull through.'

'You mean——?'

Mal inclined his dark head. 'Jeanne opened her eyes last night and recognised me. She may in a moment open her eyes again—Robert, go to your *maman* and speak to her. Let her know you are here with her.'

The boy pulled his fingers free of Glenda's and very cautiously he approached the bed. 'Maman?' He went a little nearer, and when his mother still didn't stir he cast a beseeching look at his uncle.

'Take hold of her hand,' Mal murmured.

Robert reached out and with very great care tucked

his fingers into his mother's flaccid ones. There was no reaction from Jeanne, and with bated breath Glenda stood there holding a hand to her throat. The anxious seconds seemed to stretch into hours while Glenda prayed that Jeanne would give a sign that she was aware of her son's presence.

She stole a quick glance at Mal, whose gaze was fixed upon his sister and young nephew; the unmarked side of his face was turned to her, tired lines etched deeply in the brown skin. She wasn't so much surprised by his concern for Jeanne; what startled her was the discovery that his exterior look of hardness wasn't proof that he was a hardened man. It was an armour, making him aloof, unapproachable . . . this realisation made a nerve leap against her fingertips, there under the skin of her throat. Perhaps she made a little sound and wasn't aware of it, but in that instant Mal looked across at her and his gaze seemed to go down inside her, holding her as if on a steel hook.

'You really are something of a witch, aren't you?' he said quietly.

'I—don't understand.' The words emerged in a husky whisper.

Mal moved his hand in a Gallic way, indicating Robert. 'You brought the child here, didn't you? Did you sense that Jeanne had taken a turn for the better?'

'I thought——' No, she decided not to tell him that she had feared Jeanne might be sinking and that Robert ought to be allowed to see her in case it was for the last time. 'I felt it was his right.'

'You mean you felt I was wrong to have him kept away from his mother?'

Glenda nodded, then pulled free of his gaze. 'He was fretting for her, and that was worse for him than not seeing her. I happen to know what this sort of thing feels like. I loved Edith—my own mother.'

'Ah yes—Edith.'

Glenda might have noticed a change of tone in his voice, but in that instant Jeanne opened her eyes and Robert gave a glad little cry. 'Maman! Dearest Maman, you are better!'

Jeanne lay there looking at her son with dark eyes ringed by shadows; her lips moved forming his name, and Glenda felt suddenly intrusive. With her eyes stinging she stepped outside the cubicle and walked quickly and quietly out of the unit, finding a seat in the corridor where she waited. Thank God, she thought, that Jeanne had rallied. She was still a young woman and in time, if given a chance, grief had a way of fading to a quiet acceptance of the inevitable.

A nurse passed the seat where Glenda sat and entered the intensive care unit, and she guessed that it would be only a matter of minutes before Mal came out with Robert.

She was right, and she rose to her feet as they appeared, the very tall, very dark-skinned man and the small boy whose eyes were alight again.

'I'm so pleased——' With a tentative smile Glenda took a step forward, and Robert ran to her and threw his arms about her waist, hugging her.

'I'm coming to see Maman again tomorrow and they're going to put her in a nice room all by herself, and Uncle Mal says he's going to send her lots of flowers to cheer her up. I'm so happy, Glenda!'

'I'm so pleased, Robbie, more than I can say.' She looked up at Mal. 'You've had such a worrying week—you look tired to death!'

'I feel it.' He thrust a hand through his hair, rumpling its blackness. He looked at her speculatively, as if wondering why she should care about what he'd been through this past week. The expression in his eyes was one of weary cynicism, as if he thought her concern for him was insincere. She wanted to deny what he thought; to say that she knew what it was like to sit at the bedside of someone you loved, watching the white, drawn face on the pillow and hoping some miracle might happen and death not come to seal those eyes for ever.

'I'm dead beat and hungry,' said Mal. 'Let's go and have some lunch.'

They drove to a local restaurant and lunched in the rustic garden, where there was a lazy hum of bees and a restful atmosphere. Mal ordered a bottle of Jasnières, informing her that it was a wine which was becoming rare. 'You will take a glass with me, of course?' He nodded to the waiter to fill her glass and to give his nephew Robert half a glass. 'I think you deserve it, young man, eh? For being brave.'

Robert looked pleased with himself, even though Glenda quickly said that he should have something to eat with the wine. 'We don't want you inebriated, do we?'

He grinned and sniffed at the wine in his glass. Mal suggested a *pâté* of quail with thin slices of toast, looking more relaxed as he lounged back in his cane chair and drank his wine.

'It will be a pleasure to sleep in a comfortable bed tonight,' he remarked. 'There at the clinic they provided me with a bed, but it wasn't my length, nor was it what I call comfortable.'

Glenda ran her fingers nervously up and down the stem of her wine glass and tried not to read in his

words a kind of threat. She knew he was watching her
and probably reading her mind. She was the wife who
didn't want him for a husband, but if he was in need
of being comforted, she knew he wouldn't be deterred
by a lack of welcome from her. She spread *pâté* on
toast and ate with a composure that was all on the sur-
face. The bees hummed lazily while Robert chatted
away to his uncle; to observers at other tables they
probably looked a contented trio, but all the time
Glenda was racking her brains a solution to her
problem. She could so easily have left Mal while he
was occupied at the clinic, but concern for the boy had
stopped her from leaving the man.

Mal must be aware of that! He was far too shrewd
not to have realised that she had stayed at the Château
in order to give the child the sympathy and support he
had needed so badly. Mal had demonstrated that he
had feelings . . . surely he would listen and understand
when she told him that she couldn't go through with
their marriage?

She and Robert had tender white breast of duck
roasted with potatoes and baby carrots. Mal chose a
venison casserole flavoured with brandy, and at the
conclusion of the meal all three of them had raspberries
and cream, followed by coffee, Robert's fluffy with
whipped cream on top.

The child had hardly eaten a thing all through the
week, but now there was hope that his mother was
going to pull through he had cleaned his plates and
was now sitting drowsily on a patch of grass beneath
an apple tree.

'I wish to thank you, *ma chère*, for the way you have
looked after the child.' Mal struck a match and applied
it to a thin cigar, waving the flame back and forth until

the tip of the cigar smouldered. He dropped the dead match into a saucer and studied her through a drift of smoke.

'I was glad to be of help.' Now they sat alone she felt that all her nerves were on edge, but she didn't want it to show that he disturbed her so much. No matter how hard she tried she couldn't accept the fact that she was married to him and that in the eyes of everyone, including Simon, she belonged to Malraux d'Ath.

She actually belonged to this big, dark personage, and when he looked at her, he made her feel . . . helpless. Self-anger threaded its way through her body. He was only a man, after all. He hadn't the power to strike her dead if she left him.

'It's been a trying week for all of us,' he went on. 'Not much of a honeymoon, eh?'

A quick warmth ran under her skin and she felt it coming up over her face, showing itself through her fair skin. 'We have to discuss that——'

'Indeed we do, Glenda,' he broke in softly, a deceptive softness which the sardonic look in his eyes didn't reflect. 'We've hardly seen each other and we're still like strangers, eh? As I recall, you were hardly receptive to my husbandly advances, so we're still at an awkward stage with each other.'

'Mal——' She fought to bring out the words, but beyond the screen of cigar smoke his eyes were steel hardened in ice.

'You were about to say something, my dear?' He flicked ash to the ground and kept her pinned to his gaze.

'It must be an enormous relief to you that Jeanne has turned the corner.'

'It has been a close call, *aux portes de la mort*.'

'I'm sure you willed her to get well.'

'I have a strong will, it's true.' His gaze ran over Glenda in her silk shirt and chamois skirt; a slim gold chain encircled her throat and she was plucking at it unaware.

'You'll break the clasp if you aren't careful. Why are you so nervous, *ma chère*? My sister is on the road to recovery, the sun shines and we've had a good lunch. Do I put your nerves on edge?'

'I—I can't stay with you, Mal!' The words broke through the boundary of her fear and her eyes watched him, begging him to release her with quiet dignity. 'After all, y-you have what you wanted.'

'But you haven't, eh?'

She edged her tongue around dry lips. 'Can't you be generous?'

'As generous as the Malraux family has been to Edith Hartwell for many years?'

Glenda felt her heart beating with apprehension . . . there was something in Mal's voice, something almost deadly in his regard. What did he know . . . what did he suspect?

'As you know, *ma chère*, Jeanne intended to die and so she left a letter. I haven't spoken about it to anyone and I've concealed it from the local authorities because she admits in it that she no longer wanted to live. There is a footnote to the letter; shall I tell you what it says?'

Glenda could only watch him in a dumb acceptance of what he had deduced from whatever Jeanne had written, and she knew it was about herself.

'Jeanne instructed me to ask you, my dear, who you really are.'

Glenda's heart seemed to plummet into the pit of

her stomach and suddenly she felt sick. 'W-why should she write such a thing——?'

'You tell me, Glenda—if that really is your name?'

'Of course it's my name!'

'I don't believe you.' He stared into her eyes, with their nervously flickering lashes. 'I had to be reminded that the girl who came to the Château Noir as my grandfather's guest *had green eyes*. We are all aware that these days nature can be improved upon by dyes, cosmetic surgery and contact lenses. How remiss of you, young woman, not to have invested in a pair of contact lenses that would have altered the colour of your eyes as dye has altered the colour of your hair.'

'How dare you!' Glenda felt a quick flash of temper, for at least the colour of her hair was genuine. 'I was born with hair this colour.'

'But you were not born to Edith Hartwell, were you? You might as well tell me the truth, for I'm certainly not fool enough to believe that green eyes can change to amber ones. Who are you?' He leaned forward and his eyes glittered dangerously 'Where do you come from? What became of the real Glenda Hartwell?'

'I——' Glenda shook her head helplessly. 'I knew it would happen, that sooner or later someone would guess that I never saw you or the Château before the day I—married you. I thought I could get away with it because I intended to—to leave you. I never intended to stay and go on pretending——'

'You will tell me this instant who you are.' His voice cut across hers like a sharp blade. 'Some little adventuress, eh, who got together with that woman in order to go on fleecing the Malraux estate?'

'Don't call her *that woman*!'

'I shall refer to her any way I damn well please,' he

said cuttingly. 'I can understand your sense of gratitude for your share in the very generous income that
was provided by my grandfather on condition her
daughter one day became my wife! What became of
the girl?'

'She died ten years ago.'

He drew in his breath, then emitted an angry gust of
cigar smoke. 'How did she die?'

'She fell ill while on a sea voyage with Edith.' Glenda
tried to speak calmly in the face of Mal's icy contempt.
'Edith had her buried on the island of Malta, but you
have to understand——'

'Do I?'

'Edith had been used to a life of ease and travel a-
and dressing well, and your grandfather's will only
made provision for her in relation to her daughter.
Without that income she was reduced to penury, for
she was never the type of woman to save money.'

'When did you enter the plot?' he demanded.

'Edith adopted me—I was in a children's home in
Wales. From the day she took me from that dreary
place she gave me so many nice things, and she was
always like my very own mother——'

'How very touching!'

'Oh God,' Glenda covered her face for a moment,
shielding herself from his justified sarcasm, 'I was only
a kid—I didn't realise what motivated her, and when
she eventually told me, I'd grown too fond of her to
really condemn her actions . . . and she was dying when
she pleaded with me to—marry you so no one would
guess that for nine years she'd defrauded the Malraux
estate.'

'So you admit to the fraud and that you were a party
to it?'

'What else can I do but admit it?' Glenda endured the cold hardness of his gaze. 'I can only say this in her defence, and mine, that if you had spent your childhood in a home among other children without a mother or father to care about them, then you might understand how deeply grateful a child feels when someone comes along and chooses them for a—a companion. Edith was genuinely kind to me.'

'She could afford to be, and you met most of her requirements, didn't you? You were the right age, you had auburn hair, and she obviously gambled on the fact that most people either don't notice the colour of other people's eyes or they mistake the colour. By heaven, the pair of you had a nerve!'

'I—I didn't marry you for mercenary reasons,' Glenda defended herself, looking as she sat there in the sunlight young and helpless . . . much more a victim of circumstance than the man who confronted her. How could he know how Edith had sheltered her and treated her as if she were her own dear child? With his jaw set hard like that he was obviously determined to think the worst of her . . . as if she were some adventuress.

'It—sort of happened——' she said helplessly.

'Like measles?' he asked sarcastically.

Her cheeks flushed burningly. 'I wouldn't expect you to understand—you're made of iron!'

'Perhaps you thought I was made of putty—a soft fool for you to manipulate? It must have come as quite a shock when you met me and discovered that it takes more than white skin and red hair to make me easy to handle. *Dieu*, but you're really amazing, do you know that?' He gave his head a shake, his eyes raking over her face as if seeking there the amoral look that went with behaviour such as hers.

'You have the audacity to talk of loving young Brake, yet you come to church and marry me,' Mal exclaimed. 'What sort of creature are you?'

'I—I told you—I did it for Edith.'

'My dear girl, no one is that self-sacrificing!'

'Do you have to keep being sarcastic?' Suddenly at the back of her eyes there was a sting of tears ... oh no, she mustn't cry in front of him. She had to hang on to her pride and not give him the satisfaction of thoroughly browbeating her. After all, who was he to take her to task? He'd stood in church and married her just to get his hands on a pile of turrets!

'I should think I'm entitled to be sarcastic,' he drawled. 'No wonder I was treated to all that maidenly fear, all that timid show of reluctance on our wedding night. I suppose—even for someone like you—it was somewhat intimidating to find yourself actually married to a stranger. *Dieu*, I don't know whether to think old Duval would be amused by this situation, or enraged!'

Mal leaned back in his chair, laughing low in his throat. 'Well, young woman, you've quite a lot to pay the piper, haven't you?'

Glenda gave him a mystified look. 'I beg your pardon?'

'Don't turn on the little orphaned girl act with me.' His lip curled, accentuating the scarring on that side of his face. He ground out the stub of his cigar, then laced his fingers together and rested his chin on his thumbs. 'You very well know what I mean, so we'll dispense with the play-acting. There's been enough of that!'

'But I—I don't know what you mean.' She said it

bravely enough, but deep inside her there was an acute, almost painful throb as if her body realised his meaning even as her mind rejected it.

'Do you see these hands?' He spread them open, showing the palms and then the backs of them where dark hair curled at his wrists; his fingers were long, flexible with tips that looked threatening as they pointed towards her. 'You are in my hands up to your lying little mouth, *ma chère*.' And as he said it Mal closed his hands as if, indeed, he held her there, struggling and kicking.

Glenda stared at his clenched hands and then slowly raised her gaze to his adamant face, where the scars were etched deeply in the lean cheek, pulling at the skin and giving him a sinister look. Flames had licked over that face, burning into him until every nerve in his body would have screamed with agony.

Perhaps in the aftermath of such pain he had become insensitive . . . he seemed so to Glenda, who felt sure she must look as wretchedly unhappy as she felt. She had deceived him and he had the right to feel furious with her . . . but it was the edge of ice on his anger that chilled Glenda even as the warm sun stroked her skin.

'You must despise me,' she said huskily. 'But at the time I was in a kind of daze . . . a sort of dream, and it wasn't until we went to the vestry to sign the register that I realised what I'd done. It was terrible—I felt as if my heart stopped——'

'It didn't, my dear, you merely fainted very prettily at my feet. Shock, I expect, because young Lochinvar hadn't come to your rescue.'

'Oh—you can be beastly!' she exclaimed. 'Haven't you an ounce of sympathy in you?'

'Yes, but I don't intend to waste any of it on you.

I'll concede that you wanted to save dear Edith's reputation, but at the same time you wanted the gallant
Simon to stop you. He didn't; shall I tell you why
not?'

'I'm sure you'll tell me even if I don't want to listen,'
she rejoined.

'Yes, I'll tell you, because it's about time you learned
a few facts about life. Young Brake is the type who
likes to wear a uniform and look like a knight in
armour, but when it comes to aiming his lance he just
takes a stance, like some damned statue, and decides
that caution looks braver than valour—which can hurt
like hell. And, of course, a chap has the Regiment to
consider.'

Glenda sat transfixed, outraged by such a statement,
wishing she had a lance, a very sharp one, to aim at
Mal d'Ath's heart. 'Y-you know absolutely nothing
about Simon,' she breathed, 'and you're being beastly
about him because I happen to—love him.'

'Love?' Mal arched a scoffing eyebrow. 'You
wouldn't know it if it reared up and hit you in the eye.
You're just a damn-fool girl who's got herself involved
with me, and I'm not cut from the same limp cloth as
your shiny-haired young officer, all polished metal on
the outside but no match for my kind of iron. He might
be your dream lover, *ma belle,* but I happen to be your
husband.'

His teeth, as hard and splendid as an animal's, shut
tight on the word and she just couldn't remove her
gaze from his mouth, the top lip decisively direct, the
lower lip boldly modelled . . . even rather sensual.

'But we—we have to get divorced, Mal.' She utterly
failed to keep the panic out of her voice. 'Now you
know—what you know. In a way it's a relief—I hated

the lying to you and the pretence, and I admit that I was wrong to let my feelings for Edith persuade me— Mal, why are you looking at me like that?'

Her eyes widened, the pupils expanding until there seemed just a rim of gold around them. The dappling sunlight was here and there in her hair, and her Welsh-white skin had a delicate smoothness that merged with her silky shirt, open in a vee against her throat where her slender neck-chain glistened.

'There's never been a divorce in our family,' Mal said deliberately, 'and I don't intend to introduce one.'

'Mal——' her lips quivered and she could feel nerves twisting about in her insides, 'don't play with me, please!'

'No?' His gaze played over her, with a kind of sardonic appreciation. 'The prospect of playing with you, Glenda, isn't at all daunting. I'm looking at you now and I'm not seeing that Hartwell child, I'm seeing a very attractive young woman who happens to be my wife. Do I make myself understood?'

She stared across the table at him, dark and powerful, and evoking in her the wild despair of a creature who finds itself in a trap. There was threat in the very way he half-closed his eyes, showing a glitter of steel through his black lashes.

'Let me go, Mal!' The plea broke from her huskily.

'I'm not touching you, my dear.' He spread his hands mockingly.

'Y-you know what I mean.'

'So you can go running to your gallant Simon?'

'I—I've told you I love him.'

'Yes, I remember that you told me some fancy lies.'

'They weren't——'

'You've been lying your head off, Glenda, from the

moment you stepped across the threshold of the
Château. The whole damn business has been a farce,
up until now. Now we confront each other in the raw
light of the truth; now, my Sleeping Beauty, you're
awake, and it's too bad that it isn't Prince Charming
who's awakened you. I know what my face looks like
to a woman—what it must look like to you in com-
parison to the classic profile of young Brake, but as I
told you once before, you won't see my scars when the
light is out.'

'I seem to remember,' she reminded him, 'that you
didn't like it when I asked you to turn out the
lights.'

'True, my dear, but I'm not feeling quite so sensitive
any more. Least of all where you're concerned, not
now I know you for a liar and a cheat.'

She flinched, jerking back as if he'd struck her
around the face. 'You don't mince your words, do you,
Mal? You're out to make me feel small—you're chop-
ping me down, but you won't divorce me when you
have every right and all the evidence you need.'

'Divorce is out of the question,' he said decisively.

'Why?' she asked bewilderedly. 'You've accused me
of being an accomplice to fraud, a-and you know how
I feel about Simon. What more do you want?'

'Aren't you woman enough to know?' he drawled.
'Are your female instincts so undeveloped? On our
wedding night, *ma chère,* you were telling me how
experienced you were.'

Her fair skin flushed hotly and her eyes wavered
away from his. 'Y-you can't want to—to stay married
to me, it doesn't make sense! You've got what you
wanted from our marriage—you dreamed of owning
the Château and now you have it, and control of the

business. Indirectly I've helped you, so why can't you play fair——'

'Play fair?' he broke in. 'Of all the statements you have made, Glenda, that one really takes the cake! Did you play fair when you arrived at that church, glistening in your virginal white gown and veil, playing the part of a girl who's been dead and buried for ten years? I could have had the Château and the business without any of that; all I needed was to be told that the genuine Glenda Hartwell was dead: that would have cancelled out the marriage automatically. You had to be aware of that! You can't be a total fool!'

'Thanks!' She bit her lip, and could feel herself trembling from the cruel impact of his words. 'You see everything from your angle, don't you? You won't see any of it from mine.'

'Your so-called devotion to Edith Hartwell, eh?'

'Don't sneer at devotion, Mal. The way you treat people, you're not likely to inspire a great deal!'

'I consider that I've treated you with considerable forbearance,' he retorted, 'considering the way you've led me up the garden path.'

'Up the aisle would seem more appropriate,' she murmured.

'Quite.' Behind his lashes his eyes were smouldering. 'And I intend to be compensated.'

'By me?' She tilted her chin, more with bravado than real bravery.

'By you, my dear.'

'You're refusing to divorce me?'

'Quite definitely.'

'How are you going to stop me from leaving you, Mal? Do you plan to lock me up in your tower?'

'It sounds a good idea; I might even give it some consideration.'

'Y-you want me even though you know about me and Simon?'

'He's probably held your hand a few times, *ma chère*, and he may even have kissed you, but he's too damned hidebound to have gone any further with a young innocent like you. His sort seeks out the experienced showgirl or shopgirl with whom to sow his wild oats.'

'As you did?' she shot back, infuriated by his sarcasm where Simon was concerned.

'As I *did*?' He raised a sardonic eyebrow. 'I'm not quite a doddering old fellow in need of a walking-stick. I'm thirty years old.'

'You look more than that.' She didn't care if she hurt him; he didn't mind hurting her feelings with regard to the people she cared about.

'Put it down to my scars.' His brows drew together until they met across the bridge of his Latin nose. 'They were earned in an honourable cause, if that's any consolation to you?'

'Don't think you can get round me that way——' She stopped, for his eyelids sprang up and his lashes were no longer shading the steel-like glitter of his eyes.

'Don't you dare to speak to me in that manner!' His tone of voice was as cutting as his look. 'You're an insolent little chit who needs a good spanking. You've been spoilt, my girl, by that idle, pleasure-seeking woman who took you out of a well-meaning home where you'd have been taught a trade instead of growing up to become ornamental and useless, not to mention unscrupulous.'

'How dare you say such things to me!' Glenda pushed back her chair and sprang to her feet. 'I could have walked out on you a week ago, but I chose to stay for Robert's sake. I've been of far more use to him than those cousins of yours! One of them spends her time mooning over her boss, while the other one would give anything to be in my shoes and married to you! I—I think I rather hate you, Mal d'Ath!'

'Hate?' He came to his feet in a supple movement and a stride brought him to where Glenda stood . . . as he loomed above her she backed away, into the snare of a mimosa bush. It clouded about her, scent and blossom and a feeling of helpless rage . . . she could have been well out of Mal's clutches if she hadn't felt so concerned for the child . . . she could have been back in England.

'Yes,' she panted, 'I find you utterly hateful!'

'Then we should get along fine.' His hands reached for her waist and he plucked her out of the bush as easily as if she had been one of the yellow flowers. 'I shan't have to care about your feelings, and you won't have to care about mine. One of the nuisances for people in love is that they spend so much time worrying about each other, but you and I can get on with our lives regardless.'

CHAPTER EIGHT

THERE could be no mistaking what Mal said; his words were as emphatic as the grip of his hands on her body. He meant to stay married to her . . . he wasn't going to release her.

'You—you're out of your mind if you imagine that I'm going to stay with you!' Glenda flung the defiant words at him. 'This isn't the Middle Ages, even if you do act like some *seigneur* ruling over your serfs! You can't get your servants to truss me to a tree under a pile of kindling!'

'What a very lurid imagination you have, Glenda! No wonder Edith Hartwell was able to convince you that she was the Fairy Godmother.' His hands tightened and with the minimum of effort he brought her body even nearer to his, there in that restaurant garden where other people had long since left their tables and where only the birds in the trees and the bees in the bushes made any sound. Under the apple buds the child lay curled asleep in the grass, his young mind at rest, and from a window a discreet waiter saw the man and woman locked together in what looked like an embrace. He shrugged philosophically and decided to give them another five minutes before taking them the bill . . . lovers, they lived in a world of their own.

A cynical laugh broke from Mal's lips. 'We might not live in the Middle Ages, but there are still certain people who don't care for the tarnish of scandal—a young Guards officer, for instance, with not a very large income from the family purse but with ambition to rise in the Regiment. I don't think young Brake would like it to get around that his girl-friend was really a little stray cat, adopted by a woman who used her for a fraudulent purpose. Fraud is criminal deception, Glenda. You may well have been innocent before you married me, but now you are very guilty.'

The words hung between them and there seemed nothing Glenda could say to soften the hard, emphatic look on Mal's face. He had dismissed with contempt the reasons she had given for marrying him and letting him believe that she was the Glenda Hartwell he had met all those years ago. He had scorned the sincerity of her feelings for Edith; swept aside her every argument and presented her with a very daunting one in return.

A young and ambitious officer attached to Simon's particular regiment couldn't afford to be tarnished by a breath of scandal, and Glenda saw deadly purpose in Mal's eyes.

He'd involve Simon in the scandal of their marriage if she insisted on leaving him. He'd reveal the fact that Edith had cheated and lied and betrayed Duval Malraux.

None of these revelations could hurt Mal himself . . . they could only hurt the two people whom Glenda loved.

'You'd do it, wouldn't you?' She spoke barely above a whisper, as if sharing with him some appalling secret.

'Yes.' His gaze held hers relentlessly. 'It's amazing the things we can do when we're driven.'

'Driven—*you*?' Her eyes filled with scorn. 'Your ego

can't stand it that I took you in so completely; you'd have gone on believing I was Edith's real daughter if your sister hadn't noticed that my eyes aren't green. I'm no more a person to you than the real Glenda, but you have to have your pound of flesh, don't you?'

'I'm only human.' His hands gathered her skin-close to him, as if to lay stress on his humanity. 'And you have very attractive flesh, *ma belle*, so very white and tender to the touch. How can I bear to let you go? You belong to me now, and what is mine is no other man's.'

'Is that your motto?' She kept very still, for to struggle with him would only make her more aware of his supple strength and the vigorous thighs to which he had welded her, forcing her to be aware of him through the fabric of her skirt. Damn him, but he seemed to see right through her tissue of lies about Simon. Simon had held her, but not like this. Simon had kissed her, but there had been less sensuality in it than in a flick of Mal's eyes over her skin.

Dear, dear Simon . . . he had *respected* her.

'Let's say it's our motto, my dear.' Mal prised up her chin with a hard finger and forced her eyes to meet his, just as he forced her body to meet his. 'I advise you to forget Simon Brake; just remember that if he was worth his salt, he'd have snatched you away from that altar where you stood with me: he'd have said to hell with what people thought of him. You might be making excuses for him, my girl, but deep down inside you, you're bruised because he just stood there in his speckless uniform and let you say you'd cherish me.'

Mal gave a mocking shake of his head. 'It's what they call keeping a stiff upper lip, eh? No doubt he's very good at that; I'm better at other things, and I say it in all immodesty.'

'You——' she swallowed air to relieve the pounding in her chest, 'you're beyond description! I loved Edith, but I—I'd have run to the ends of the earth if I'd known what you were like! You're no—gentleman!'

'And you're no lady, my dear,' he mocked. 'You're a stray waif whom the shrewd Edith picked up on her travels. I don't imagine you have a clue about the identity of your real mother——'

'I can't help that.' Glenda gave him a hurt look. 'Kick the stray out if you think she's such a mongrel.'

His fingers gripped her chin and he scanned her face, with its delicate yet detailed bone structure beneath the skin that was white but not pallid or sickly. Her eyes watched him with a kind of wariness, amber as a cat's and set at a slanting angle beneath the slim brows . . . a Celtic face framed by the dark red hair which had attracted Edith Hartwell's attention in the first place.

'Where will you go if I kick you out?' he asked.

'As far away as I can get from you,' she retorted, hoping against hope that he would relent and let her go. 'After all, Mal, what sort of a marriage could we hope to have—together?'

'It will be interesting to find out,' he drawled. 'Now go and wake the boy while I pay for our lunch——'

'Mal,' her eyes filled with pleading, 'have a heart!'

'You said I was made of iron, *ma chère*, so how can I have a heart?' He pushed her away from him, mimosa pollen streaking her hair. 'Wake Robert—we're going home.'

'It isn't my home—it couldn't ever be!'

'Then let it be your damned prison, *madame*.' He

turned away from her, a hand reaching into his pocket for his wallet. 'I'm sure I couldn't care less!'

Glenda gazed after him, seeing a kind of imperious power even in the way he walked . . . that he was justified in his judgment of her was mortifying; she was guilty as accused and he was in the right to punish her. With some men it might have taken the form of a beating, but Mal was more subtle than that. He had struck where the damage wouldn't show but where it would certainly be felt.

Oh, Simon . . . her fingers clenched upon a spray of mimosa and wrung the delicate flowers off the stem. Her heart cried out for help, but she knew that if she dared to follow her silent cry with a vocal one, via a long-distance telephone call, Mal would do as he threatened and involve Simon in this wretched business.

Mal was in a rage, it smouldered deep inside him and it wouldn't take much to make him boil over. All that he had wanted had been his all along, and he was infuriated because in addition he found himself with a wife he didn't want . . . not as a person.

But a wife was a woman . . . she could give him what an ambitious man also wanted, a son to crown his achievements.

A son to grow up as heir to the Château Noir and the Malraux Ironworks.

Glenda glanced wildly around her, as if seeking a way to escape him. She could run, but Mal had the car and he'd drive her into a ditch before he'd let her get away from him . . . a vixen with a hound at her heels.

Mal wasn't the courteous, disciplined gentleman that Simon was. Mal was a man who had been robbed of much of his boyhood by a grandfather who had welded him and all his hopes to the ironworks, until he lived

and breathed the smell of ore. It seemed to her that it
ran molten in him, steelplating his feelings.

'Don't stand there daydreaming!' His voice broke in
on her thoughts, and when she looked in his direction
he had lifted Robert out of the grass and the boy
nestled there in his arms without fear. Glenda followed
them to the car and slid silently into her seat. Mal
drove along the golden lanes that led back to the
Château, rising there against the sky in all its silvery
enchantment.

It stood as if spellbound, wrapped in the somnolence
of the afternoon, amid the sun-drawn scents of the
woods that sloped to its stone walls. The sun gleamed
in the Gothic windowpanes, those that peered from
the swathes of dragon-green ivy cloaking the mach-
icolated towers.

'The turrets have witches' hats on them.' Robert had
stirred awake and was kneeling on the back seat with
his arms entwined about Glenda's neck.

Mal gave a short laugh and flung a side-glance at
Glenda as they drove into the forecourt. 'A fit place
for a witch to live in, wouldn't you say so, Robert?' he
asked.

'Is he talking about you, Glenda?' the boy wanted to
know.

'Yes, Robbie, your uncle has a peculiar sense of
humour.'

'I don't think Glenda's a witch, Uncle Mal,' the boy
said solemnly. 'They have warts on the ends of their
noses.'

'Don't you be so sure, my boy.' Mal brought the car
to a smooth standstill. 'Beware of those with eyes like
a ginger cat; they're the ones you can't trust. They're
the ones that twist and twine about a man, and turn

his head back to front if he isn't careful. The golden rule, *mon enfant*, is to keep your head well screwed on your shoulders so you won't go losing it over a female. You'll thank me for some sound advice when you are grown up.'

Robert eyed his uncle in an old-fashioned way, then he pressed his nose against Glenda's neck. 'I like girls,' he said. 'They smell ever so nice.'

'All part of the witchery, *mon ami*.' Mal leaned there lazily, watching the way the boy embraced Glenda.

'Mal, do stop trying to disillusion Robbie,' she protested.

In an instant Mal's gaze was levelled upon her face. 'I'm merely trying to pass on to him my own hard-learned lesson, my dear.'

'Oh, but I'm sure you'd agree that females as wicked as me aren't all that thick on the ground,' she dared to taunt him. 'I'm sure Robbie isn't likely to meet a sinner like me.'

'What's a sinner?' the boy wanted to know.

'A liar and a pretender,' Mal replied.

'Oh——' Glenda caught her breath painfully; she had no defence against the truth, but it seemed unnecessarily cruel of him to say such a thing in front of the child, unless it was his intention to turn Robert against her? Was that to be part of her punishment? She studied his dark, sardonic face but couldn't be sure of what he intended. There was a tiger-like unpredictability about him.

'It doesn't sound very nice, does it?' he said. 'You'd like to deny it with those lovely, lying lips of yours, but you know you can't.'

'Mal, please——' She flicked her gaze pleadingly in the boy's direction. 'It's between us, isn't it? Say what you like when we're alone, but——'

'But let others go on thinking you're angelic and sweet?'

She flushed hotly. 'I've never pretended to be an angel, and I'd hate to be labelled sweet. You just won't believe that I—I sometimes allow my heart to rule my head.'

'Don't we all,' he drawled, 'at some time in our foolish lives!'

He swung out of the car and opened the door beside the back seat. 'Out you come, my young man. Pleased with yourself now you've seen Maman and seen for yourself that she's going to get better?'

Robert slid from the car and stood there thoughtfully. 'Why did she try to do that—thing to herself, Uncle Mal? Why did she want to die?'

'Sometimes, *mon ami*, it isn't that we want to die, it's that we have no reason for living. It can happen to any of us. *Le bon Dieu* failed to make the perfect human being, and one suspects that such a creature would be an appalling bore.'

'When will Maman come home?' Robert wanted to know, reaching out for his uncle's hand. 'They won't make her stay in hospital a long while, will they?'

'She'll have to stay until she's quite better, *mon ami.*'

'I see.' Robert nodded to himself, then his gaze travelled upwards to the tower where his uncle's private apartments were situated 'Can I go on sleeping up there?' he asked.

'No, I think the time has come for you to return to your own room,' Mal said firmly. 'You are a big boy now, aren't you? You understand that Glenda and I wish to live alone in our part of the Château? It's what married people do.'

Robert glanced at Glenda, but she couldn't answer his look of appeal; her heart seemed as if it had come into her throat, as it does when shock jolts the body. She had somehow taken it for granted that the boy would go on sharing the Tour Etoile until his mother came home, but one look at Mal's face disillusioned her.

'Glenda?' the boy murmured.

'I—I'm sorry, Robbie, but your uncle makes the decisions.'

'I'm glad you realise it,' said Mal.

'You're mean!' Robert pulled his hand free of his uncle's and ran up the front steps and in through the door which one of the staff had just opened. Glenda went to follow him, but Mal caught her by the elbow and detained her; she glanced up at him, tense as a wire. 'As a matter of fact, the child's grandparents are coming over from America and I've agreed that Robert can go and stay with them for a month or two. Jeanne needs some form of psychiatric treatment and there's a rather good place in Paris where I think she ought to go. I should have arranged it before she became so depressed that she attempted suicide. I allowed business to come before anything else, and the matter of our—marriage.'

He paused upon the word and searched Glenda's face with a thoroughness such as she had never known before. 'Dammit, why didn't I remember that child's green eyes!'

'Mal, for God's sake——!' Glenda tried to break free of his grip, but his fingers tightened, bruising her flesh. His eyes glittered down at her and the scarring made a savage mask of his face.

'It's accomplished,' he said through his teeth. 'We

are man and wife whether we want it or not, and I will say this for you, Glenda, you're devilish attractive, and there's a side to me that isn't cast iron.'

She caught her breath audibly, and a taunting smile lifted the edge of his lip. 'And don't give me any more lies about your physical experiences with Brake—do you think I can't tell that you've never slept with a man? Once it's happened the look in a woman's eyes changes—she becomes aware. I look in your eyes, my dear, and they're very unaware.'

'So long as you can bear to—make love to a woman who cares nothing for you,' she said defiantly.

'I'm sure it won't be unbearable.' He put his free hand to her cheek and stroked his fingers down to her neck and the lobe of her ear; suddenly he bent his tall head and put his lips where his fingers were. 'I'll make you forget your soldier boy,' he said against her ear, his breath fanning inside, warm and yet sending little shivers through her body.

'Simon has my heart——'

'*Ma chère*, that sounds like a bit of dialogue from a magazine story. Having your heart isn't going to do him much good; I'm sure he'd sooner have what I've got—your virginal white body.'

'You—you're horrible,' she said, a catch in her voice.

'Of a surety,' he mocked, 'I'm truly a monster, and I have the face to prove it.'

'Oh—it isn't your face, it's your attitude!'

'I think my attitude quite reasonable, Glenda, when all is said and done. I'm the injured party.'

'I think you're enjoying yourself—like some cruel boy who's trapped a fly in a bottle!'

'And you think I'm about to pull off your wings?' he taunted. 'Your opinion of me is most unflattering—I feel quite hurt.'

'I doubt if I could hurt you,' she retorted. 'I think your feelings are well protected.'

'A man's feelings need to be, with girls like you around. So innocent-looking, so almost vulnerable, and yet you do an audacious thing such as marrying a stranger. I'd be almost tempted to admire such nerve— if I wasn't the man involved. You must have had misgivings when you met me and realised how different I am from the stiff-upper-lip Englishman whom you claim to be madly in love with.'

'As you've an English side to you, Mal, perhaps I hoped that you'd be—gallant.'

'A quixotic fool, don't you mean?'

Her gaze flickered away from his, which was so disconcerting and so direct. He seemed to look right into her, searching her out as no one else had ever done. It was as if he wanted to strip her bare, body and soul. It was a thought that made her tremble.

'Stop twitching,' he ordered. 'The web you're tangled up in was woven by your own hands; you set out to deceive me and now you have to live with me. You had better make the best of it—I certainly intend to.'

'Y—you leave me in no doubt of that!'

'I hope not a shadow of a doubt, *ma belle*.' And so saying he pulled her roughly close to him and brought his mouth down hard and demandingly on hers. Her lips were forced to yield . . . she had no strength to pit against his power and felt herself go weak in his arms, a sensation such as she had never felt before and quite unlike the weakness of going without food, or the fragility that follows a bout of 'flu. It was somehow more strangely fluid, as if the very centre of her was melting away.

Suddenly it terrified her and she tried to break away from him. 'No!' his lips seemed to snarl against hers and his grip was close to being savage. 'Oh no, I'll have none of that—you're mine now and you're going to stop thinking about the gallant Captain Brake; you're going to stop pining for his handsome face and his courteous attentions. You're going to get all you've asked for, my girl. I'm the man you married!'

There was no denying it . . . this big, dark, domineering man was her husband and he had every right to kiss her, to hold her, to take possession of her.

Helplessly she gazed up at him, and suddenly he swept her up in his arms as easily as he had lifted Robert. 'Once again I carry you over my threshold, my darling,' he mocked.

Up the steps he strode and in through the doorway; the sun was setting through the Gothic windows of the vaulted hall and the streaks of gold and flame seemed to burn across his scarred features. With his black plume of hair and his bold nose, his eyes sheened by temper, he made Glenda think of a pillager who meant to have his way with her.

He stood there in the centre of the great hall, legs straddled as he held her, a man who from a boy had hammered metal and handled iron and whose eyes seemed to smoke with those hot fires.

'Look around you, Madame d'Ath. You and I will share all this, and if you ever let another man touch you, then I shall break your neck and the courts will call it a crime of passion. Understood?'

No, she didn't really understand him. Her life with

Edith hadn't prepared her for someone like Malraux d'Ath, who with his mixed heritage had an approach to life that was neither English nor truly French.

French shrewdness had ruled out English sentimentality and replaced it with a kind of implacable logic; they were married, so they might as well live together ... he didn't seem to regard love as important.

'Haven't you ever loved someone?' she found herself asking him.

Up went that sardonic eyebrow, and then he slowly slid her to her feet. 'What do you mean by love, I wonder?' His hands stayed on her hips, their warmth and firmness penetrating through the fabric of her skirt. 'Some romantic ideal, eh? Tristan and Isolde, Dante and Beatrice, Jane Eyre and Mr Rochester.'

'I wouldn't have thought you even knew about such couples,' she said, trying not to be aware of his hands clasping her hips. 'You probably regard them as romantic fools who wasted too much of their time caring about each other. You probably lavish your affections on wrought-iron gates and balcony grilles.'

He laughed briefly and his hands made a stroking movement that made her catch her breath. 'You may have something there, Glenda. There certainly is a difference in the handling of iron and the handling of a woman. I'll take you to the works one of these days; you might be interested to see how the Malraux iron is manufactured. It's going to be part of your life now— as I am.'

'Y—you've made up your mind——?'

'About you, Glenda?'

'About—us?'

'*Mais oui, madame.*' His voice was faintly taunting,

but the set to his jaw was adamant. 'My mind is quite made up on your staying at the Château Noir; this is where you belong and this is where you are going to live—with the man you married!'

'Then——' her lips quivered, 'I'm not to be forgiven?'

'If by forgiven you mean sending you back to England, no.' His voice and his look hardened. 'Some would say that I'm meting out a punishment that isn't too harsh, but no doubt you regard it as terrible that the husband with the unlovely face is insisting that you live with him. Think yourself lucky that I'm not insisting that you—love me.'

'Love you?' she echoed.

'Don't faint, my dear.' The sun had fallen out of the sky and the hall had filled with shadow, but not quite enough to hide the glitter of Mal's eyes. 'I shall ask for everything but that, rest assured.'

She gazed back at him wordlessly. Didn't he realise that when a woman had to give a man everything but her love, then she gave him nothing, and had nothing in return?

Footsteps struck the paving of the hall and it was one of the servants come to light the big wrought lamps on their chains. As the switches clicked and the lamps filled the hall with light, Glenda pulled free of Mal and turned blindly away from him. She felt helpless and dazed, and then saw that a tea trolley was being wheeled into the library. She followed it on shaky legs and found Aunt Héloise dozing by the fire; she sank down in the companion armchair and held cold hands to the warm blaze of the logs. When the sun went down into the valley the evenings turned chilly in the spring-time, and it reminded Glenda of home to be able to sit beside a cheerful fire with a cup of tea.

At the rattle of the teacups and spoons Aunt Héloise stirred awake. She gazed across at Glenda's pensive face. 'All was well at the clinic?' she asked. 'You did not find Jeanne any worse?'

'Oh no,' Glenda said quickly. 'She's very much improved and is being moved out of the intensive care unit into a room of her own. It seems as if she'll now make a good recovery.'

'*Le bon Dieu* be praised! It was a foolhardy thing to do in the first place, so let us hope she has learned a lesson she won't forget. You may pour the tea—I don't take sugar, which is disgusting stuff and no good for anyone. I will have a couple of those Marie biscuits.'

Glenda poured their tea and was glad that Mal didn't join them. She quite liked his aunt, a woman too concerned with the state of her own health to be bothered to interfere in other people's concerns. Edith had been a non-interfering type of woman and Glenda thought it the best way to be. She had no time for those who tried to run other people's lives; who felt they had some kind of divine duty to criticise the way other women wore their hair, chose their make-up and their clothes. It was as if they wanted everyone in a kind of uniform chosen by them; do this, do that, but never please yourself what you do!

Edith had never imposed her tastes upon Glenda, who had grown up to appreciate those who didn't meddle. It was an invasion of privacy to meddle in the lives of other people. Everyone was entitled to their own foibles, and their own likes and dislikes.

It was this reserve in Glenda that made her shrink from the authority that was so much a part of Mal. She felt as if she was going to be absorbed by him, and there seemed nothing she could do but accept his dictation.

'Is there something troubling you, Glenda?'

She had been staring into the fire, her cup of tea neglected, so that when she shook her head Aunt Héloise looked unconvinced by her denial.

'You may tell me, child. I've been a wife and I know that marriage can be a mixed blessing. Mal is treating you in a satisfactory manner? I am not being inquisitive, but you no longer have a mother of your own to whom you can turn for advice.'

'You're kind, tante, but I don't need any advice.'

'Then you are fortunate. I only know that when I was first married I found that the realities of living with a man were far different from the romantic ideas I had harboured. Men are different from us, and I don't mean in the obvious way. They think differently. They approach a subject from a more logical point of view and don't always understand that women can be more sensitive and take to heart a remark, a look, an intonation of the voice which seems to the woman significant when all the time it is a mere bagatelle. Believe me, child, a man's skin is thicker in more ways than one. He doesn't always realise that some little dart may have penetrated deeper than he meant it to. Mal, he has said something a little unkind to you, and you brood over it?'

'Some of his remarks can be a little barbed, can't they?' Glenda said quietly. 'I—I don't know whether he means to hurt, or whether he doesn't know that he's hurtful. Has he always been so—hard?'

Aunt Héloise dabbed at her lips with a napkin. 'He came very much under the influence of my father to whom the family business meant everything. It was a great disappointment to my father that he had daughters instead of sons, so that when Malraux was born he put pressure on my sister to let the child be reared in France, here at the Château. As things turned out, of course, it was just as well that my nephew and niece were permitted to live here rather than in Algeria. When those terrible troubles blew up in the North African colonies it was suicide for Europeans to remain there, but my brother-in-law, Mal's father, had put his heart as well as all his money into the plantation there and it came as no real surprise when he and my poor sister became victims of the rebellion. Had the children been with them, then their lives would have been lost as well. As you can imagine, Malraux was drawn into every aspect of the ironworks, and he developed a genuine ability and ambitions to expand that delighted Duval Malraux.'

The old man's daughter paused there and gazed reflectively into the fire before glancing back at Glenda with a rather cynical smile edging her lips. 'It has to be said about my father that his reasoning could often be as convoluted as some of the iron that came out of the foundry, that was why his will was so unreasonable. Even from the grave my father wanted to dictate to Mal, who would not inherit what he had been taught to cherish unless he carried out every injunction in that will. Something not easy for a strong-willed young man to do, not in this day and age when the arranged marriage has become outmoded and young people are practising free choice.'

The arthritic hands moved expressively. 'A woman of my years is perplexed by the attitudes of the young, especially in this matter of free access to each other's bodies, which can't be too healthy! However, times change, if not always for the better, and I think it understandable if Malraux is sometimes a little impatient with a wife which another man imposed upon him. He is not too unkind, eh? He has had all this worry imposed upon him by Jeanne's hysterical behaviour, so you can't expect him to be always the attentive lover.'

'I don't expect it—I don't want——' Glenda bit back the words, for she was an innately loyal person and Mal was her husband . . . he really and truly was the man she had married, and she had never been more conscious of the fact. She couldn't bring herself to blurt out to his aunt that she didn't want him to be her attentive lover . . . that all she really wanted was to leave him so she could go and love a man called Simon; who put her at her ease and didn't make her feel so on edge when he entered a room, when he looked at her . . . particularly when he touched her.

Such a confession would shock his aunt; it was obvious from the way she spoke of Mal that she respected him and felt a fondness for him. In view of having a son of her own in the family business it might have been quite reasonable if she had harboured a grudge against Mal, now the man in charge of everything.

'I know what is going through your mind.' His aunt smiled a little wearily. 'Had Mal not married you, then my own son would have inherited the estate and the works. I'm glad that he didn't '

'But how can you—his mother—say that?' Glenda gazed at her wonderingly; would she ever begin to understand this family?

'Don't mistake me, child. Matthieu is my son and I love him, but he did something that nice but rather weak men have a tendency to do—he took a selfish, complaining, dissatisfied wife who would have liked nothing better than to be mistress of the Château Noir; and had Matthieu inherited the larger portion of shares in the business, that wife of his would have poked in her nose and things would have gone terribly wrong—she would have caused trouble between my son and my nephew. As things are now, she can do nothing, except of course make Matthieu's life miserable with her constant dissatisfactions. There is nothing I can do about that, except hope that one day he'll have the gumption to leave her.'

'They have no children?' Glenda asked.

'No, and it's just as well. Women of her type are not cut out to be mothers. I have noticed you with the young Robert. You will make a kind young mother, and Malraux is the sort of man to want a family. He has a natural sense of responsibility and was good enough to let me come and live at the Château. That daughter-in-law of mine would have seen me put into a home for the elderly—she is a cat, that one. I warned Matthieu, but he wouldn't listen to me. Nowadays I say nothing, and when he comes to see me he comes alone, thank heaven.'

'It must worry you, *tante*, that your son isn't happy in his marriage,' Glenda said sympathetically.

'You will learn yourself, child, that worry and motherhood go together, but of course without the tears we wouldn't enjoy the smiles, would we? Most of life is a mixture of them and they make us aware that we are alive, that we are human and will make mistakes as we go along the various roads which we either choose for ourselves, or have chosen for us. Your road has been chosen for you, admitted, but bear in mind, when Malraux is a little brusque in his manner, that he can also be a very considerate man. I am witness to it, child. Without hesitation, when my health began to fail he offered me my own apartment here at the Château; my own flesh and blood allowed his hands to be tied by the *peignoir* strings of his wife.

'So be it.' Aunt Héloise spread her hands speakingly; hands that must once have been slender and attractive but were now swollen-jointed, her rings bedded into her fingers. 'As one gets older, one accepts the inevitable.'

'I—I'm having to accept it while I'm young,' said Glenda, her voice husky with emotion.

'You mean that you came to your marriage without love for Malraux?'

Glenda nodded. 'I didn't realise—all the implications.'

'Ah, but you surely understood that such as he would not be content with a marriage in name only? Was it that, child, that you hoped for?'

'I don't know what I hoped for, *tante*. I went through with it—like a child playing a game, or an actress playing a part. When I woke up to the reality of it all, it was too late to call it off.'

'But you don't quite—dislike him, do you, *ma petite*?'

Glenda gazed into the hot heart of the fire and saw again his tall and demanding figure, his scarred profile, and the smouldering deep in the steel grey of his black-lashed eyes.

'He dislikes me,' she said huskily, and before she could stop herself she poured out the truth to his aunt, who was somehow rather like Edith, to whom she had always been able to talk. There had been no secrets between them and the only time Edith had betrayed her was in this matter of the Malraux marriage. She had trusted Edith to get her out of it, not knowing until the last that it was the last thing her adoptive mother wanted. The marriage had been necessary . . . for everyone but Glenda herself.

'My good gracious!' Aunt Héloise clutched a hand to her heart. 'And my nephew knows of this—deception?'

'Yes.' The leaping fire revealed the wan whiteness of Glenda's face. 'Jeanne realised that I wasn't the original Glenda and she—she told him of it in her suicide note.'

'Ah, so she left such a note; he has not said and now the reason is in relation to you. It was *très méchant* of you, child, and very daring in the circumstances. He's a man of temper! No wonder you sit there in apprehension, but I think in your place I would have fled from him while the chance was there. All last week he was with Jeanne and absent from the Château— whatever made you stay when you felt so in fear of him?'

'The little boy needed me—oh, I don't want to sound holy and righteous,' Glenda added hastily. 'I like Robert, but it also seemed—seemed a way of making recompense. I'm not just the adventuress Mal thinks I am. I've never cheated anyone before, b-but Edith was dying and she'd been so good to me. What was I to do?'

'You could,' his aunt said drily, 'have told him the whole story before you embarked on marriage with him. Then he would have respected you, but now you have made him suspicious of you. At the best of times, *ma petite*, men rarely understand women, so just think what his thoughts must be when he looks at you and sees an artless girl, but knowing all the time that the same girl has lied to him, deceived him at the very altar, and landed him a partner in a marriage contract which became null and void when the real Glenda died a decade ago.'

Aunt Héloise slowly shook her head at the white-faced girl in the firelight. 'You have my sympathy, child. What more can I say?'

'Would you try and make him understand that I—I'm not as bad as he thinks?'

'No, Glenda. I made a vow when I came to live under my nephew's roof that I would never interfere in his life. I've kept that vow and I won't break it. It is for you to work things out for yourself, child. Leave him, if all you are going to find with him is retribution.'

'He's refused to let me leave——' Glenda caught her breath. 'He wants me here so he can go on punishing me—he says if I leave, then he'll publish the fact that Edith accepted money from the Malraux estate knowing that she wasn't really entitled to it. If I thought he was just threatening me, then I'd go, but he means what he says. He does, doesn't he?'

'Knowing Malraux I have to say that he probably does mean his every word. A man of honour likes honour in others, otherwise he can be a very ruthless man. Yes, you are locked in a dilemma, my child, and the key to your release doesn't lie in my hands. I am sorry.'

It came as no surprise that Mal's aunt was on his side; it had been a forlorn hope that she might intercede and attempt to soften his obduracy, perhaps even persuade him that the marriage was best annulled.

'I will have no part in a predicament you've brought upon yourself,' Aunt Héloise reiterated. 'But I will

offer a piece of advice you might be wise to follow . . .
there is a way for a woman to make a man unbend and
that is in the boudoir. Think on it.'

Which was exactly what Glenda didn't want to do
. . . to think of herself and Mal in that most intimate of
places!

CHAPTER NINE

MAL's behaviour in the next couple of weeks was baffling to Glenda; except for curt greetings at mealtimes he seemed to ignore her presence at the Château Noir.

His threats were held in abeyance and this increased her sense of uncertainty rather than relieved it. It was as if he was lulling her into a false belief that their marriage, after all, was to be one of those in which a couple dwelt under the same roof but without any physical contact.

She didn't know what to think or believe, and each morning she awoke alone in the big fourposter bed and told herself that Mal was unpredictable as the tiger stalking its prey. He'd wait and watch to see if she was fooled by his waiting game, and then he'd pounce on her. She grew more and more certain of it, for there had been no intimation that he was going to allow her to get used to him and his surroundings. No, this was all part of her punishment, this cat-and-mouse game!

Trepidation was her companion on her rambles about the Château. She found much of it fascinating, some of it beautiful, but never for a moment did she feel at home.

She entered its rooms as if she were a visitor uncertain of her welcome, sat in its deep windowseats where the long curtains partly concealed her and felt like an intruder who had come in from the street and would be thrown out if discovered.

There were plenty of books to read, glass-fronted

cabinets full of them, and thanks to the education which Edith had bestowed upon her Glenda could read as well as speak French without any effort. There were paintings all along the galleries and some of them were Italian and others Dutch, teeming with colour and detail. There were attics beneath pepperpot turrets where old toys were stored, outmoded costumes and all manner of bric-à-brac which in its time had been played with and treasured by members of the Malraux family.

Hoping to learn something of Mal's earlier years, Glenda studied some old photograph albums which she found on a shelf in one of the attics. He was in some of the photographs as a boy, mainly in the company of a tall, dark-moustached man who she decided was Duval Malraux, for he had a look of command which he had passed on to his grandson. She was disappointed to find that Mal had ceased to pose for the camera after about the age of sixteen, but the lean and rather serious face gave her some idea what he must have looked like before that accident at the foundry.

She glanced curiously through a pile of records with sentimental titles and wondered who had chosen them. She tried to picture Mal being carefree and debonair on the dance floor, a girl in his arms whose blonde head would barely reach his broad shoulder.

Why did she think of him in association with a blonde? Was it because he was so dark . . . oh, it was nonsense, of course, to try and fit him into the mould which suited Simon so well. There had never been two men so dissimilar, and sitting there on a shabby leather hassock, her cheek streaked with dust, Glenda opened a battered little box and released the tinkling music of a Brahms waltz.

She imagined the little brocaded box being played in a nursery, then suddenly closed the lid before the music evoked images which she couldn't bear to face. There wasn't a moment when she wasn't nervously alert for the decisive footfall that was Mal's, for the deep tones of his voice ... she knew that one night soon she would see the looming darkness of him in the doorway of her bedroom. He would look at her with steel-cold eyes, and reach for her with unloving hands. He would make her have his baby, and she couldn't bear to think of it happening in that way.

She pushed the music-box out of sight, but the tune still jingled in her brain so that she ran down the twisting stairs as if trying to run away from the music. Reaching the last few stairs, she tripped and almost fell, and clung there with a fast beating heart.

A shadow loomed over her and there was Mal, breeched and booted.

'What have you been doing?' he demanded. 'You have a dirty face—have you been up in the attics poking around?'

'Yes.' She pressed herself against the stair rail, feeling as if the strength drained from her legs.

'There's only a lot of old lumber up there, it should be cleared out. I'm about to have morning coffee—come and join me.'

She walked beside him, almost shockingly aware of his vigour and the tang of horse clinging to his breeches. The strong fingers of the hand nearest to her were clasped about his riding crop. 'What's so interesting about the attics? Why moon about up there when you could come riding with me?'

She gave him a surprised look. 'You never ask me to go with you.'

'You never ask to come,' he rejoined, as they entered the *petit salon* where coffee and sandwiches awaited him. He went to the table, took a sandwich and hungrily ate it. 'Come and pour out for me.'

As she did so he watched her, handing her a handkerchief in exchange for his coffee. 'Wipe your face and tell me why you go up there.'

She turned to face a wall mirror and rubbed the dust from her cheek. 'It's just something to do.'

'I suppose you miss being with the boy?'

Glenda nodded. Robert's grandparents had taken him back to Boston with them and he was expected to stay there until his mother was well again. Jeanne hadn't yet been discharged from the local clinic, but when she was pronounced fit enough Mal was going to fly with her to Paris where she would become a voluntary patient at a small hospital which dealt with psychiatric problems. This time Mal was firmly resolved that his sister should undergo treatment for the depression and despair which had led to her attempt to kill herself.

'I'm informed that Jeanne is being released from the clinic on Friday,' he said, and waited for Glenda to sit down before he lowered his big frame into a chair whose chintz fabric made him look even more lusty. His shirt had pulled open across his brown throat and his skin showed a sheen of sweat from his vigorous ride.

'Is she coming home to the Château?' Glenda asked.

He shook his head. 'I thought it best if I took her straight to Paris on the midday flight; coming back here will only remind her of things best forgotten, and she's agreeable to going directly there. I shall spend the weekend in Paris . . . would you like to come?'

The invitation was so unexpected that Glenda was

lost for a reply. She hadn't given it a thought that he might ask her to go along and she almost said she would go. Paris was a beautiful city . . . a romantic city . . . was that what he had in mind, that in Paris he would consummate their marriage?

'I'm waiting for your answer, *ma chère*.'

Her lashes flickered and she glanced away from him. 'No, I don't think I'll come, thank you.'

'May I be permitted to ask why not?' That slightly pleasant note left his voice. 'Are you so well travelled that you can afford to be blasé about a trip to probably the most cultivated city in the world?'

'It—isn't that——'

'Then I presume it's me? You don't fancy being in Paris with me?'

'I'd only be in the way—you're going there to put Jeanne into a hospital—and you have to remember, Mal, she doesn't like me very much.'

'Jeanne knows how well you've looked after Robert.'

'That's the trouble, Mal. You know what she thought, that I wanted to take Robert away from her. I—I think it's best if I don't come.'

'What if I insist that you come?'

'You wouldn't— —' Glenda looked at him and saw from the obdurate set of his jaw that he would if he felt like it. She saw the rampant strength in his shoulders, the narrowed danger of his eyes. He didn't love her, so he was capable of anything . . . his heart would never warn him not to hurt her.

'I wouldn't advise you to bet on it.' Suddenly he was standing up and his stride brought him to where she sat. His hand reached for her shoulder and she winced. 'You wouldn't turn down Paris if dear Simon was asking you to go; you don't want to go with me, do you?'

It was defiance more than courage that made her brave. 'No,' she said, 'I don't want to go with you.'

'Then to hell with you!' He let go of her shoulder, swung on his booted heel and strode from the room. Glenda sat there and it was many minutes before her heart stopped pounding. Oh, how much longer could she fight him off? Surely soon her body would beg of her mind to let him have his victory ... perhaps she should even get it over with, go to him, give herself to him, and settle for peace rather than this constant combat that wounded both of them.

She drew up her legs and curled herself into a ball of dejection. She had caught the hurt look in his eyes ... he thought she didn't want to be seen with him because of his scars. But it wasn't that. What made her repudiate Paris in his company was that it was a city made for lovers. Its very balconies with their beautiful ironwork seemed to be a setting for people in love, who wanted to look at the stars and see them reflected in each other's eyes.

Paris in the springtime, with the boulevard tables set out under the chestnut trees, uninhibited couples holding hands across the wine glasses.

Suddenly Glenda felt a wetness on her hand and realised that she was crying like a person in a dream. She reached into her pocket and found the handkerchief which Mal had given her to wipe her face; she wiped away her tears and smelled the cigar smoke on the linen. She breathed it and felt a strange lurch of her heart ... what on earth was causing her to have these odd symptoms? A touch of conscience? A stab of guilt because she didn't dare to believe that Mal was just being nice to her and had no ulterior motive in asking her to go to Paris?

She came to her feet, her eyes still pricking, and felt an impulse to go and find him; to say she didn't want him to think his scars had anything to do with her reluctance to go.

Several minutes later she found him in the smithy at the rear of the stables, stone-arched and redolent of smoke. He was stripped to the waist and working the bellows that fanned the forge to red heat. He glanced up as she came and stood in the doorway and there was a cold lack of expression in his gaze ... a look which she had learned was deceptive. Deep down in those eyes there was always tinder that could smoke and blaze in a split second, so she was on her guard.

'I've had enough of squabbling with you for one day,' he said, his tone of voice matching his look. 'Go and poke your little nose somewhere else.'

'Mal——'

'What is it, my sweet? Have you had an attack of sudden affection for me?'

'You always have to be—sarcastic!'

'Don't tell me you'd like me to try being something else? Forgiving and tender, perhaps?'

'I—I thought you might forgive me——'

'Am I hearing you correctly?' He placed a hand to his ear. 'Are you actually taking the blame for something?'

She flushed and her eyes wavered from his. 'I think I would like to come to Paris—I didn't want you to think, Mal, that I'm put off by your scars.'

'Magnanimous of you, *chérie*. I'm quite overwhelmed by your generosity in quenching your distaste, but I wouldn't want you to make such a sacrifice on my behalf and I won't take you up on your offer.'

'You mean you don't want me——?' Her words trailed off and she felt a hot wave of humiliation sweep over her . . . fool, fool that she was, she might have guessed that he'd throw a refusal back in her teeth.

'How does it feel,' he softly asked, 'to be rejected?'

'You—you should know!' she shot back at him. She turned to hurry away, but with that silent elasticity of his he was after her before she had taken a dozen steps. He spun her around as if she were a doll, his eyes seething in his scarred face as he swept her off her feet and flung her across his bare shoulder.

Silent and swift he strode with her among the trees, furiously crossed the courtyard and bounded up the steps of the Tour Etoile. Glenda clung there against his hot bare flesh and knew that he was fuming; her head spun and her heart was frantic with fear. The breach she had hoped to heal had gaped wider and was filled with the fire of Mal's anger . . . hair and limbs disordered, she was flung on her back on the bed he had not yet shared with her.

Now he meant to share it and she knew it, and against such strength and temper she had no chance. Her dress was ripped away and her underclothes were torn in his fingers like tissue paper. Her pleadings fell on deaf ears, and she struggled in vain as he held her pinned to the bed with his right hand, using his left to position her.

'You have been asking for this,' he said, teeth gritted, 'ever since you came to the Château, and bear in mind, *madame*, that it didn't have to be this way!'

'No——' She choked his name as his body came down on hers, crushing and hot and uncaring of hurting her. Now it was happening, now there was no way for her to stop it, she wished she knew how to lie there cold and supine and make him her rapist instead of the husband who took what was his due.

As the pain bit deep, Glenda lost control of herself and her teeth sank into Mal's shoulder and drew blood. '*Dieu!*' His eyes were hot steel on her face, and then his face came down to hers and hid its scars in her red hair as the passion surged from him . . . wave upon wave.

The room was still and dim, and the day had waned, lost in a brazen sky that was now dusky.

Mal stirred and his heavy arm lifted away from Glenda, leaving coolness to waft across her body. He raised himself on his elbow and looked down at her, at the pallor of her face, her eyes wide open, her lips closed now and bruised by the kissing.

'I'm not going to say I'm sorry,' he said in a sombre voice.

'As if I'd expect it.' The words came languidly from her. The dimness in the room surprised her . . . they had been here for hours and she had believed that it was quickly over and best forgotten. It had not been like that at all. She had thought he would go on making mad, angry love to her until she died of it.

She could feel his smooth, sweat-sheened hip pressing hers, his hard leg flung across her legs. Her breath caught in her throat.

'Your lies are well proven, aren't they?' His breath wafted across her face and she could just see the hard white glimmer of his teeth.

Glenda knew what he meant . . . he had wrung from her the pain of initiation so he knew that Simon had never possessed her. That was the word to describe it, of course.

Where Mal was concerned it was the only word.

He flung away the bedcover and slid from the bed. He flexed his arms, then studied the dial of his watch. 'Ye gods, have you any idea what the time is? It's eight o'clock! It's dinner time and, by hell, I'm ravenous!'

When she said nothing and the word ravenous hung in the air between them, he abruptly leaned down to her and cupped her face in his hand. 'You all right, child?'

'Hardly a child any more, Mal,' she rejoined.

'You damn well provoked me, you know that, Glenda.'

'I know it now, Mal.'

'And I've given you grounds for a divorce I could hardly defend.'

'Divorce——?'

'A husband is no longer allowed by law to rape his wife.' With these words he left the bedroom, and left her lying there with his words drumming in her brain.

Mal and Jeanne left for Paris on Friday as planned; Glenda didn't suggest again that she go with them, and Mal didn't ask. In the day and night before he left he didn't approach her again as the demanding husband. His face at mealtimes was a withdrawn mask which gave nothing away, and when on Friday he went to collect Jeanne from the clinic he bade Glenda *au revoir* in a remote tone of voice.

She watched the car drive away and felt almost a sense of abandonment. She couldn't forget, or dismiss, what had happened between them, but he seemed to have done so, and being relatively innocent about the male attitude towards sex she could only suppose that what had seemed overwhelming to her had been but another sensual experience to Mal.

Glenda was still feeling the effects of those time-submerged hours in his arms. She had been a virgin, and the extent of his passion had left her bruised as well as emotionally churned up. When she was alone she found her thoughts filled with that afternoon.

Because so much of her time had been spent with Edith she hadn't given much thought to sex, except to suppose that it was just another of those functional acts of life that created children if a couple wanted them but wasn't anything exceptional . . . least of all in the way poets wrote about it.

Now she had undergone her initiation into that world of the senses . . . now she knew exactly what happened, and when she thought of what Mal's body had done to hers, and when she thought of those gasping little cries he had wrung from her, her cheeks grew hot. Her flesh still seemed to feel the touch of his hands, and then it was as if her bones were melting away and she had to sit down until her strength returned.

How, she wondered, would he spend his time in Paris after he had seen his sister settled into her private room at the hospital? He was no stranger to that disturbingly romantic city; he probably knew several women there and might feel the urge to renew one of his friendships. Would he go out dining with one of those smart, sophisticated women, and afterwards would he take her to bed and be as passionate as he had been the other afternoon?

Glenda could see it all in detail, and she sat there amid the lime trees of the Château garden, amid the oleanders and the damask roses that were as heavy on their stems as if made from velvet, and felt as if a knife twisted in her insides.

She envisioned him with that other woman, gowned

by a Parisian dressmaker, an expensive perfume clinging to her skin, beautifully groomed hair framing an
enigmatic type of French face. She would lift that face
to Mal, unafraid of the scars that somehow intensified
his male power, and he would bend his tall head and
mould his lips to the red lips offered. They would kiss
on an iron-framed balcony, and then with that easy
strength he would lift her into his arms and carry her
into the shadows of a boudoir where she would allow
him to pull the zip of her dress all the way down to the
bottom of her spine.

And he would kiss her there, as he had kissed
Glenda. There would be no place where his lips wouldn't
go, and in the warm darkness the woman would cry his
name and he would laugh softly, like a tiger purring its
contentment as the permitted hand stroked its haunches
and felt the silk-smooth fury and strength.

These were thoughts such as Glenda had never had
before, and they made her want to keep to herself so
that on Saturday, when Renée invited her to a local
fête, she made an excuse not to go.

'You'd enjoy yourself,' Renée persisted. 'With Mal
away, and in Paris of all places, you're entitled to have
a little fun yourself.'

'Why did he not take you?' Rachel lowered her
newspaper and gave Glenda a curious look. 'Didn't he
want you to go with him?'

'In the circumstances,' Glenda shrugged evasively.
'Jeanne hasn't taken to me as a sister-in-law, has she?'

'Oh, Jeanne is not quite in her right mind,' said
Renée, spreading apricot jam on a piece of toast. 'She
wouldn't be going to that place in Paris if there wasn't
something mentally wrong with her.'

'Poor Jeanne isn't crazy,' Rachel said sharply. 'She

did what it isn't always wise to do, loved a man madly. If you become that involved with another person and then lose him, then there can't be a lot left to look forward to.'

'But Jeanne has Robert.' Renée gave her sister a wide-eyed look. 'You always insist that I'm the romantic one, and now you're talking in a romantic way. What has brought this on, sister dear?'

'Common sense, as a matter of fact.' Rachel poured herself another cup of coffee. 'Love isn't really all that romantic, is it? It's too real, too hurting at times, and too fundamental, to be anything like a magazine story. Love is passion, of the body and of the spirit. You can see how it tore Jeanne in half when Gilles was killed . . . that's love, if you can take it.'

'The way you put it, I don't think I'd want it,' Renée argued. 'I'm not going to believe that being in love is all doom and gloom; I think you were born looking on the dark side instead of the bright. I'm sure Glenda agrees with me.'

Rachel glanced across the table at Glenda; the three of them were taking breakfast on the veranda of the morning room, beneath a rather uncertain sky. Now and again the sun broke through the clouds and washed the veranda with an intermittent brightness.

'I have a feeling,' said Rachel, 'that Glenda is in agreement with me rather than you, Renée. Glenda knows what I mean.'

'Do I?' Glenda spoke reservedly.

'You should.' Rachel's look was sardonic, giving her a look that was extremely Malraux, 'You are crazy with love yourself, aren't you?'

Glenda abruptly pushed back her chair. 'I have to go and write a letter, so please excuse me——'

'Aren't you coming to the *fête*?' urged Renée. 'I want to introduce you to my boss.'

Glenda shook her head. 'From the look of those clouds it's going to rain, and *fêtes* are awful when that happens, with everyone crowding into the refreshment tent and smelling of damp hair and flannel trousers.'

'You spoilsport!' Renée pouted.

'She's being moody,' Rachel drawled. 'Love takes you that way when a girl's husband is in Paris. Who knows who he sees and what he does? I wouldn't allow a husband of mine to be on the loose in Paris.'

'When do you propose to get a husband?' Renée asked. 'You're a born career woman, and men aren't keen on them.'

'Perhaps so.' Rachel shrugged. 'I shall have a first-class career instead of a second-class man ... damn you, Glenda, for being a nice, vulnerable sort of girl. It would make me feel too guilty if I tried to take Mal away from you.'

Glenda stood there riveted. 'Well, that's being candid!'

'I know.' Rachel gazed directly up at her. 'Is he as exciting in bed as I imagine him to be?'

'Rachel!' There was a genuine look of shock in Renée's eyes. 'How can you ask such a thing?'

'Enviously, dear sister. Anyway, it proves to Glenda that I've never slept with Mal, doesn't it?'

'I never thought you had,' said Glenda, recovering.

'Oh, and why not?'

'Instinct.'

'About me, Glenda?'

'No, about him.'

Glenda walked quickly from the veranda and she could feel herself shaking with emotion. She wasn't exactly angry with Rachel . . . but what Rachel had done was to put into words what she had been afraid of even thinking.

She couldn't be crazily in love . . . not with Mal.

In the depths of the Château garden there was a summerhouse almost smothered in mauve and orange wallflowers, and there she went, taking her writing-case with her. She sat down in a cane chair at the little round cane table and opened her writing-pad. She gazed out of the summerhouse doorway at the trees, whose leaves were rattling a message that rain was on its way.

She'd write to Simon and tell him she was coming home to England and did he still want her? Mal had mentioned divorce; he had implied that he wouldn't try to stop her any more.

Dear Simon, she wrote, and then the pen fell listlessly from her fingers and suddenly she was outside the summerhouse with her face pressed to the wallflowers whose scent was so heady as large spots of rain began to fall upon the thick scarves of petals.

Mal, beat her heart. *Mal,* hold me and be with me as you were . . . oh, as you were!

She shook with the wanting of him . . . the rain came down harder and beat against her longing body. Why deny any more that those hours with him had been heaven on earth . . . there had been no one but Mal in her heart and in her arms that long afternoon. His kisses had swept away her girlhood longings and replaced them with a woman's needs. His touch had brought a rapture she hadn't dreamed of, and she was possessed by him even in this moment, even as she stood in the rain in his garden and he was somewhere in Paris . . . perhaps with someone else.

She shivered bleakly at the thought and realising

how wet she was, went back into the summerhouse. She sat there watching the rain beat down on the trees and the scent of the wallflowers wafted in . . . memories of her wedding day came back to her and now she knew that it had been inevitable that she come to love the tall man with the cruel scars. The spell had been cast there beneath the stained-glass windows . . . for love was a kind of enchantment.

There were shades of dark as well as gold in the crucible in which the elements were blended to form the mysterious gem called love. The gem was set into the heart and sometimes it glowed warm with passion and caring, and at other times it pierced the heart with pain.

It was pain that Glenda was feeling right now. Mal had gone away believing that she didn't want him . . . oh God, she had never wanted anyone so much! She ached with the wanting . . . the very thought of his lips on hers sent wildfire racing through her veins.

Was it too late to make him want her too . . . as someone loved . . . loved with all the strength and power in that big body?

Glenda leaned back in the cane chair, closed her eyes and listened to the rain on the multitude of leaves. The birds made twittering sounds in their hideaways and if it were possible the flower scents were headier. She had slept hardly at all in the night, and it would bring a little relief from her thoughts if she could doze off here in the solitude of the summerhouse.

She must have dozed, and it had to be a dream when a tall figure walked into the summerhouse and stood looking down at her. She was aware of him there, but she didn't dare to stir, to come awake, or he would vanish into those realms where dreams were lost.

'Glenda,' his deep voice made something special of her name; a deep voice with a slightly foreign intonation. 'Are you asleep?'

Her lashes fluttered and lifted and still he was there, tall against the clouded daylight, wearing the beige suit and brown shirt in which he had gone to Paris.

'No,' she sat up, her eyes wide open now, 'I'm not asleep!'

He leaned down to her, looking deep into her amber eyes. 'I was tempted to kiss you awake, but a kiss from me might have been the last thing you wanted.'

'No,' she said again, 'I mean—*yes, oh yes, please kiss me*!'

In one movement, without any effort, Mal lifted her out of the chair and held her against him, her feet suspended from the ground. His mouth crushed hers and where their hearts met there was a violent pounding. 'I couldn't stay away from you,' he breathed, his hand stroking her hair. 'I saw Jeanne settled into the hospital and then booked a flight back to you . . . all I could think of, *chérie*, was being with you and loving you. How I want to love you, until it is driving me crazy! *Mon amour, ma bien-aimée. Je t'aime, je t'adore.*'

Glenda sighed with joy, her arms wrapped closely about his neck, her fingers deep in his black hair. 'Oh, Mal, is this really true? Pinch me or I just won't believe it.'

'There are things I want to do, my love, but pinching you is not one of them.' His lips moved hungrily over her face, and then he kissed her eyes. 'Thank *le bon Dieu* you are the girl with the amber eyes . . . the other one was not for me, but you are. Tell me, am I still the damned ironmonger you cannot love because you imgine you love the soldier boy?'

'In some ways Simon is nicer than you, but you are
Mal . . . you are Mal.'

'You said that as if you meant it.' Hungrily he held
her, welded to him as if he never meant to let her go.

'Of course I mean it.' Her eyes on his face were as
hungry as his arms around her. She touched his face,
stroked the ridges of his scars and then put her lips to
them and gently, gently kissed them 'I could have died
when you left for Paris without me.'

'I shall never go anywhere without you again,' he
promised. '*Dieu*, I thought you hated me for what
happened that afternoon, but once I started I couldn't
stop. I've never known myself so ravenous for a woman
. . . you brought out the devil in me, do you know
that?'

'I always knew there was a bit of the devil in you,
darling, but I think there's a bit of an angel as well.'
She studied his dark and ravaged face. 'Am I forgiven,
Mal?'

'Entirely, *ma chère*. I forgave you when you lay in
my arms, so sweet and warm and passionate.'

'Was I passionate?' Her eyes pleaded with him.
'You're so much a man, Mal, that I couldn't bear to be
disappointing for you.'

He laughed softly, making that purring sound that
sent fire-tipped little thrills through her body. 'What a
day this is! Shall we go and make ourselves cosy in our
tower!'

'I'd love it,' she confessed.

And holding her like his booty . . . his beloved booty,
Mal d'Ath carried home his bride.

Harlequin® Plus

A WORD ABOUT THE AUTHOR

"I am a true spinster of romances," says Violet Winspear, "for in the old days, the word spinster meant 'a woman who spun,' and in the writing of a story, one spins and weaves and forms a pattern that it is hoped will prove pleasant and also satisfying."

Violet Winspear has been spinning Harlequins—both Romances and Presents—for more than twenty years. Many of her novels have had decidedly "devilish" titles—such as *Lucifer's Angel* (Romance #593), *Devil in a Silver Room* (Presents #5) and *Dearest Demon* (Presents #130).

But whatever the title, readers know that when they pick up a Violet Winspear book they will be transported to an exotic locale: a Spanish courtyard, a tropical grove, an Italian *piazza*. What they probably don't know—although the writer isn't shy about revealing the secret—is that her most colorful spots reflect London's markets and streets.

For Violet Winspear, a true Cockney, grew up in the East End of London, an area particularly hard hit during World War II. Perhaps it was the wartime trauma, she reflects, that made her realize her "need to hide from the harsher realities of life." The delighted response to her first book taught her that many other people need this escape, too. "They need also," she claims, "to believe that love is a far better thing than hate."

Today Violet Winspear lives in a small bungalow at the English seaside. It is here she spins and weaves her warm and human stories of romance.

Just what the woman on the go needs!

BOOK MATE

The perfect "mate" for all Harlequin paperbacks

Traveling • Vacationing • At Work • In Bed • Studying • Cooking • Eating

Pages turn WITHOUT opening the strap.

Perfect size for all standard paperbacks, this wonderful invention makes reading a pure pleasure! Ingenious design holds paperback books OPEN and FLAT so even wind can't ruffle pages – leaves your hands free to do other things. Reinforced, wipe-clean vinyl-covered holder flexes to let you turn pages without undoing the strap...supports paperbacks so well, they have the strength of hardcovers!

SEE-THROUGH STRAP

Built in bookmark

Reinforced back stays flat.

BOOK MARK

BACK COVER HOLDING STRIP

10" x 7¼", opened.
Snaps closed for easy carrying, too.

Available now, send your name, address, and zip or postal code, along with a check or money order for just $4.99 + .75 ¢ for postage & handling (for a total of $5.74) payable to Harlequin Reader Service to:

Harlequin Reader Service

In U.S.
P.O. Box 22188
Tempe, AZ 85282

In Canada
649 Ontario Street
Stratford, Ont. N5A 6W2

Name _____

Address _____ City _____

State/Prov. _____ Zip/Postal Code _____

Offer expires May 31, 1983

30156000000

Now's your chance to discover the earlier
books in this exciting series.

Choose from this list of great

SUPERROMANCES!

SUPERROMANCE

Complete and mail this coupon today!

- -

Worldwide Reader Service

In the U.S.A.
1440 South Priest Drive
Tempe, AZ 85281

In Canada
649 Ontario Street
Stratford, Ontario N5A 6W2

Please send me the following SUPERROMANCES. I am enclosing
check or money order for $2.50 for each copy ordered, plus 75¢
cover postage and handling.

☐ # 8	☐ # 14	☐ # 20
☐ # 9	☐ # 15	☐ # 21
☐ # 10	☐ # 16	☐ # 22
☐ # 11	☐ # 17	☐ # 23
☐ # 12	☐ # 18	☐ # 24
☐ # 13	☐ # 19	☐ # 25

Number of copies checked @ $2.50 each = $_____
N.Y. and Ariz. residents add appropriate sales tax $_____
Postage and handling $_____
                        TOTAL $_____

I enclose _____
(Please send check or money order. We cannot be responsible for cash
sent through the mail.)
Prices subject to change without notice.

NAME_____
                    (Please Print)
ADDRESS_____APT. NO._____
CITY_____
STATE/PROV._____
ZIP/POSTAL CODE_____
Offer expires May 31, 1983   3015600000